The Skipping Verger
And Other Tales

John Reid Young

Cover and illustrations

By

Annie Chapman

ISBN: 84-615-9632-3
ISBN-13: 978-84-615-9632-4

For Beatriz, William and Oliver

CONTENTS

PUBLISHER'S NOTE

ACKNOWLEDGEMENTS

My mother, Annette, will probably be smiling down from up there so I'm sure she won't mind my thanking her more than anyone else, mainly for passing on her enjoyment for telling a story. She was also very kind in allowing me to adapt two of her own stories for this collection.

I would also like to thank Annie Chapman for her beautiful illustrations and for immediately understanding what I had in mind.

My thanks also to Cliodna O'Flynn and the Island Connections Newspaper for their kind support and encouragement, and to Romina Torres at the Tenerife News Newspaper for her assistance in making this book printable.

THE SKIPPING VERGER

Santa Cruz was a busy port on a bright sunny morning in early December 1932. The fish stalls were crowded with flinging arms and shrieking women, haggling with clients over the best of the morning's catch. Cheerful men, unhampered by women's duties, were carrying bunches of tenderly wrapped bananas aboard one of the Yeoward ships which was bound for Liverpool. A fat German Hugo Stinnes vessel was unloading South American timber. Meanwhile a magnificent Union Castle liner was being nudged gently into place against the South mole by a pair of muscular tugs.

She was the lavender-hulled Carnarvon Castle on her way to South and East Africa from Southampton. One of her passengers was Dr. Hugo Simpson, an eccentric and irritable Oxford geologist. He was accompanied by his quiet, young assistant, Angus.

Their aim was to stay for a period of two months in Tenerife investigating volcanic rock formations at the base of Mount Teide. Dr. Simpson was believed to be the owner of one of the largest collections of rock samples from around the world and he was particularly anxious to add to his trophies one of Tenerife's gems. This was a blue, sub-volcanic, hydrothermal sample to be found close to Mount Teide.

They anticipated using the Monopol Hotel in Port Orotava as their headquarters. It was advertised in Brown's Guide to Madeira and the Canary Islands as a first class family hotel, with a lovely view up to the peak of Mount Teide and the only one in the valley with hot and cold water laid on to the bedrooms. It was owned and run by a German couple, Andreas and Erna Gleixner, but British visitors were always made very welcome indeed. Its large, airy rooms overlooked the sea and the town's pretty fishing harbour was just a stone's throw away. Afternoon tea was served in a central Spanish patio and it had its own terraced garden. Most importantly to British gentlemen visitors, the hotel guaranteed good wines and cigars.

Unfortunately, already showing further signs of his fastidious character over breakfast, the doctor began to feel very unwell indeed soon after stepping off the gangway.

Whilst they waited for their transport on the mole it became clear they would not be travelling as far as the Orotava Valley that day. In fact they were advised to make a brief halt at the cathedral town of La Laguna. They had been informed by a fellow British traveller, who decided not to invite them to stay at his house on the slopes above the capital on account of the geologist's nature, that there was a very excellent English-speaking doctor in the old town.

By the time they reached La Laguna, high up on a plateau nearly eighteen hundred feet above sea level, Dr. Simpson was feeling so indisposed that he was barely able to move without being embarrassingly sick. He was also shivering with cold.

They took rooms at the Aguerre Hotel, on the recommendation of a Mr. Hamilton, the shipping agent who came aboard to welcome the ship. Once the Bishop of Tenerife's residence, it had been turned into a comfortable hotel in 1885 by a fellow countryman called Benjamin Renshaw.

The Spanish doctor came almost at once to attend to the English visitor. He could hardly have been kinder but teased Dr. Simpson with his honest opinion. Naturally it did not amuse the foreigner to be told that he had probably been poisoned by the English food aboard a British ship! The kind Spaniard, who introduced himself as Dr. Valerio Luz, suggested rest for a few days before resuming their journey, and that the doctor should drink gallons of *manzanilla*, sweetened camomile tea fresh from the herb garden at the Aguerre. The hotel's cook also sent him half a *papaya* on the following morning. The fruit is well known as a remedy for almost all ills. Whether it was the tea or the papaya, or the generous and kind attention they received, which was typical of islanders, Dr. Simpson and his temper made a steady recovery and they stayed in La Laguna for just four days.

While the doctor lay in bed Angus kept him company, sitting at the window overlooking the street below. He was required to read extracts to

Simpson about the history and traditions of Tenerife as well as from earlier scientific papers written by previous foreign explorers of the Canary Islands.

Although the young assistant had begun to find the geologist a touch demanding, this enabled him not only to feel the sun on his face but also to observe a very quaint sight that very afternoon soon after lunch, when most local people appeared to be enjoying a siesta.

Angus was gazing out of the window up the deserted, cobbled street just enjoying the colours when he noticed a rather thin looking gentleman in a black suit and wearing a wide-brimmed black hat appear from a doorway and walk in their direction.

It was not an ordinary walk. The man was not moving in a straight line. Nor did he walk at a steady pace. Instead he zigzagged down the street, often stopping and suddenly jumping forwards, sideways or even backwards as if to avoid a puddle. Then, just as he passed directly below the hotel window, the thin man with the black hat stopped abruptly. There, like a soldier on the parade ground, he did a right sharp turn and literally skipped to the other side of the street.

The solitary gentleman then proceeded to walk briskly in a straight line for at least fifty yards before jumping and zigzagging again towards the church, *La Iglesia de la Concepción*. Naturally this episode greatly improved the poor assistant's outlook on life and Angus was unable to contain a certain amount of hilarity. Nevertheless his outburst of laughter failed to amuse Doctor Hugo Simpson in the least. His last wish was that he, and especially his assistant, should find something even the slightest bit funny.

Just after lunch on the following afternoon, with the geologist still grumbling very ungratefully in bed, Angus again sat at the window. He saw the man with the black hat come out of the same doorway and make his way down the street towards the hotel and then on to the church. Sure enough, instead of walking as any ordinary man would, he zigzagged and skipped and hopped in a most eccentric manner all the way to the church, following more or less an identical pattern as he had done on the previous afternoon. Angus did not want to upset the doctor again so he just smiled to himself and continued reading. Actually the man with the black hat had clearly worried Angus and, like any young scientist, he determined to discover the cause of the man's strange walk.

His need to ascertain the reason for such eccentricity became even greater when he spotted the man in black walking down the street again on the following morning, this time when it was full of people carrying out their daily business. What is more, on this occasion, although the gentleman again made his way towards the church, he took an entirely different route. He skipped and turned almost exactly under the same buildings but at opposite sides of the street to that he had done on the two previous quiet afternoons. If at all possible, the odd behaviour appeared even more apt for scientific research by the fact that the man with the black hat was greeted by almost every passer-by and he returned their courtesy by raising his hat and then promptly leaping like a gazelle over some invisible object.

The next morning a completely recovered Dr. Simpson and his assistant were due to depart for Port Orotava and they breakfasted early. After most generous helpings of fruit, bread and magnificent cheeses, while Angus was in the doctor's room making certain everything was neatly packed, he peeped out of the window to discover that it had begun to rain quite heavily. He was just in time to see the man with the black hat coming out of his doorway as usual, this time opening a black umbrella. Angus waited to see what would happen. He was very surprised and rather disappointed, as a matter of fact. His eccentric gentleman walked briskly down the street towards the church in a perfectly straight line. He didn't even skip or leap when greeted by passers-by.

The excellent Dr. Luz came to the Aguerre Hotel. He wanted to see Dr. Simpson and Angus on their way personally. It was another very kind gesture and Angus took the liberty of enquiring about the man with the black hat.

"Oh!" replied the doctor with a reassuring smile. "That is Antoñito, our *sacristán*, the church verger. He has been an assistant at the church since he was a boy," he explained.

"As you have observed, he is quite a character. To be precise, we like to say he is very artistic. He skips and jumps to avoid standing on the shadows in the street. You see, he does not want, let me say, to destroy their perfect expression. For him, when the sun shines, every shadow is an example of art produced by the effect of nature on the earth, and upon man's industry. He believes every shadow is a work of art by God. He takes this very seriously, as you have seen!"

For an instant Dr. Simpson stared with a blank look in his eyes and appeared unable to utter a word. Angus was not certain if his employer had been stymied by his young impertinence or by the Doctor's very unscientific explanation. For a moment, he actually didn't care. He was much more impressed with the doctor's fascinating logic than about his geological investigations with Dr. Simpson. Indeed, whether it had anything to do with the remarkable skipping verger or not, young Angus became ordained as a priest a few years after returning to England.

THE BANANA LORRY

When I was a boy in the 1960s we lived in a small house on the edge of a banana plantation in the Orotava Valley. I had a best friend who lived in the big house in the middle of the plantation.

His name was Manolito, which rather suited him in a Spanish kind of way because he was skinny, incredibly charming and mischievous. But he also tended to be ill rather often as a result of his asthma. My mother felt sorry for him because he had lost his own mother when he was only five.

Until I was sent to boarding school in England when I was nine I spent every minute of the day with him and our favourite pastimes were hunting lizards, rather cruelly I'm afraid, making home-made boats to float on the big irrigation tanks and helping the men in the banana plantation. Manolito's father was a very important man in the valley and owned the plantation. People referred to him as *El Conde*, so I presume he must have been a Count. I liked him because he played tennis with my father at the British Games Club and let me watch television with Manolito. We didn't have a television.

Manolito was my best friend for most of the year. In the summer his father always put him onto the mail boat which sailed to the island of Fuerteventura. He used to stay there for two long months with his mother's younger sister, Aunt Marina. He would come back coloured like a chestnut and with not a trace of asthma, after spending every hour of the day in the sea or exploring the sand dunes. Except for his adoring father, Manolito loved his Aunt Marina more than anybody in the world. Her free spirit and kindness contrasted plainly with his strict Catholic schooling and his father's inhibiting depression. She was possibly one of the very few bohemian aristocrats on the islands. To the astonishment of her family in

Tenerife and to the delight of gossipers, Marina lived in a cottage on the Jandía peninsula with an artistic German gentleman, until he suddenly disappeared one day.

One late November day after school, Manolito and I were watching the banana plantation men having their lunch under the shade of a jacaranda tree. They were discussing all the work they would have to do that afternoon, chopping down bunches of bananas and loading them onto the lorry for them to be taken to the ship the following day. Most of *El Conde*'s bananas were shipped to the mainland but some ended up at Covent Garden or Liverpool.

Before beginning their afternoon labour the men had time for a siesta. Celestina, the cook at the big house, called down into the bananas and gave us a plate of rice with fried bananas and eggs which we ate with the maids in the kitchen. My mother always knew that if I didn't turn up for lunch at home I would be eating with Manolito and the servants at the big house.

"Did you hear what Vicente said?" asked Manolito as we edged down the water trough to the field where the men had begun chopping bunches. "He said the lorry is taking the bananas to the ship in Santa Cruz."

When Manolito began to explain his plan I understood why he had been so unusually quiet over lunch. He wanted to go to his Aunt Marina on the Jandía peninsula. If he could get onto that banana lorry it would take him to the ship which would undoubtedly go to Fuerteventura. He made me cross my heart I would not say a word, but he needed my help. It was a daring game and I was in.

Just before sunset the men began rolling up the banana bunches for transport, as usual in grey-blue blankets, and stacking them gently onto the old, green Dodge lorry.

It was a simple, well worked out strategy. Just as the fourth row of rolled up bunches of bananas on the back of the lorry was about to be completed I carried out my orders. I rolled about in apparent agony on the earth, crying that I had been stung by an *alacrán*, a small, black species of scorpion, feared and often warned about in gruesome tales, but very rarely sighted in the Canaries. The men immediately jumped down, shouted contradicting advice and flung their arms about in a wild frenzy. My natural acting skills distracted them long enough for Manolito to slither down from the jacaranda tree like a snake onto the back of the lorry, where he grabbed one of the blankets, wrapped it round himself and filled the last gap left in the incomplete row. He was perfectly disguised as a bunch of freshly cut bananas. I ran home clutching my innocent sting and forgot all about the adventure until the front door bell rang just as we were having supper.

It was Manolito's father. He was using his blue bandanna to mop beads of sweat which were cascading down his forehead. His usually calm and measured voice shook and I remember his handsome face was a kind of grey colour and contorted with anxiety. My mother gasped when he explained that Manolito had disappeared. My father glared down at me as I was questioned. Had I played with Manolito today? Where did I last see him? Had we been digging another tunnel under the banana plantation? We had dug one earlier that year and it had caved in on us. Did we play anywhere near the water tanks today? He feared the worst and I sensed trouble.

"He's gone to live with his Aunt Marina!" I said after a long, thoughtful silence. I told *El Conde* that

Manolito wanted to go back to Fuerteventura and had got onto the lorry which would take him to the ship.

"But these bananas don't go to Fuerteventura. They go to Barcelona!" said Manolito's father, finding certain relief in my ridiculous explanation and even permitting the beginnings of a sympathetic smile.

What neither I nor Manolito had known was that before being shipped anywhere the bananas were taken to the packing shed close to the botanical gardens. That was where bunches were cut up into *manillas*, hands of between fifteen and twenty green bananas, and put into boxes for export. Andrés, the chauffeur, drove *El Conde* to the packing shed immediately.

They found Manolito curled up in the lorry's cabin under the same blanket he had used to disguise himself with. He was cold but his smile betrayed a mixture of pleasure and mischief, and his father could only punish him with a long, tight embrace. There was much more happiness to come. The following summer *El Conde* decided to take a holiday himself and accompanied Manolito to Fuerteventura. Whilst my best friend explored the dunes and learnt to fish, his father took long walks along the beaches on the Jandía peninsula with his departed wife's younger sister. He evidently fell in love with Marina, for he brought her back to the Orotava Valley and they were married shortly before Christmas.

THE OTHER PASSENGER

It was late February in 1936, there was a damp north westerly breeze blowing into Puerto de la Cruz and it promised more rains.

The British Vice-Consul was settling in to his regular afternoon game of bowls at the British Games Club when a message was sent down saying there was an urgent matter for him to attend to. In fact the office driver, Siverio, was waiting for him in the car park. He handed over a small brown envelope with the consular seal on it. Inside was a concise message from Mr. Patterson, the Consul in Santa Cruz, which said "It seems we are getting Franco. Please keep your ears to the ground".

He had heard about the troubles in Madrid where the head of the armed forces, General Franco, had tried to put pressure on the provisional government to annul the election results and to declare martial law. But the latest information received by the Foreign Office, and passed on to him by the Consul, was interesting and possibly bad. It meant the islands were being sent a source of mischief. Nevertheless, these were troubled times and the ideological battles going on in Madrid, with a little help from the communists in Russia, were also being carefully monitored by British

Intelligence.

Earlier that month Franco had sent a communiqué to all his military chiefs saying that they were now in a state of war. What he meant was that, for the good of Spain, they ought to prevent the red rot taking hold. In other words he was suggesting they should participate in a military coup. The proposal failed because the Civil Guard refused to be a part of it. Shortly afterwards, Manuel Azaña was sworn in as president of the new Republic and, fully aware of the plot, decided to move the conspiring generals away from sensitive military regions like Zaragoza, Valencia and Oviedo. The information from British Intelligence suggested that General Franco was being sent to the Canary Islands as Commander General of the forces in the islands.

Having lost his position as Chief of Staff and upon receiving his orders to part for the Canary Islands immediately, the General naturally understood he was being exiled. He therefore quickly arranged for a secret meeting with other generals, including Generals Mola and Goded. They agreed that they should prepare a coup d'état to be captained, as soon as everything was prepared, by General Sanjurjo who was at the time himself exiled in Portugal.

By all accounts General Franco played his cards

very close to his chest and then appeared almost too cautious for action from his headquarters in the Canary Islands. Without ruling out playing a part in future conspiracies, Franco would not commit himself.

The British Vice-Consul in Puerto de la Cruz was a very discrete gentleman and yet very much in touch with ordinary civilians. The family firm gave work to many local islanders and a very special relationship had been built up over the years. He was a highly respected and liked man. Close ties had also been established with the wealthy and aristocratic members of the local Spanish community, many of whom were active members of the British Games Club, a very colonial institution in its heyday, and most of whom were considered close friends. So he was well placed to sense or detect any developments. He reported nothing unusual in the coming weeks. Folk on the street appeared oblivious of high manoeuvres. They remained as peaceful as ever, but hopeful of better conditions promised by the new government. There was, however, a growing and natural sense of alarm amongst landowners at the prospect of radical left wing politics gathering strength in Spain.

But by the end of June 1936 the coup was practically ready and General Franco must have been convinced because British Intelligence reported that high level, secret negotiations had taken place for the hire of an aircraft which would be used to clandestinely fly Franco across to Morocco, from where the military coup would be launched. The London correspondent for ABC, the right wing Spanish journal, had been instructed to hire an aeroplane, a de Havilland DH 89 Dragon Rapide which had in fact belonged to a member of the British Royal Family.

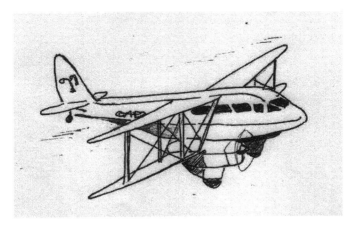

The twin engine aeroplane was to be flown to Biarritz. From there it would hop over to Lisbon and then refuel at Casablanca before heading for the Canary Islands. So as not to raise any suspicion on its arrival at Gando Airport in Las Palmas the plane would be carrying three passengers, Mr. Hugh Pollard, a retired British Major and ex-Secret Service agent, his daughter Diana and a friend of hers called Dorothy Watson. In return for taking the risk and for passing on an obscure message, "Galicia salutes France" to a local doctor, they were offered a free holiday in Puerto de la Cruz. The old port had become an attractive destination for well to do British travellers.

It appears, however, from information discovered in a diary belonging to a local source, that there might have been another passenger on the aircraft. Early in July 1936, just five months after receiving that initial brief note from the Consul concerning Franco's transfer to the islands, the British Vice-Consul in Puerto may have received further instructions, this time not through the usual Consular channels. It is possible he was requested to provide temporary accommodation for the other passenger and to ask no questions. From then on everything seems to have occurred very quickly.

A Spanish looking gentleman with an English name arrived carrying a good size brown leather over-night bag and was shown to his room.

It was late evening on 15th July. The Dragon Rapide had arrived at Las Palmas on the 14th, the same day on which leading monarchist politician, José Calvo Sotelo, was assassinated in Madrid, prompting a more determined and hasty attempt for a military coup. On the morning of the 16th the guest departed early, soon after being served breakfast and even before the Vice-Consul's wife took her early morning stroll through the rose garden.

Leaving his over-night bag at the foot of the bed he told the lady of the house that he was going to play golf at the Peñon Golf Club in Tacoronte and that of course he would be delighted to dine with them that evening. The Peñon, a club with a very British feel to it, had been opened in 1932 and at the time was only the second in the whole of Spain.

The other passenger, presumably the Spanish looking gentleman with the English name, never returned for dinner. In fact he simply disappeared. A few months later, if it hadn't been for the brown leather over-night bag which the Vice-Consul's wife had stored in one of the out rooms, it was almost as if the other passenger had never existed and had just been a figment of someone's imagination. Nobody ever enquired about him and the Vice-Consul carried out his instructions to the letter. He asked no questions. Nevertheless, there had been a great deal of excitement, especially when the military rebellion began, and he heard rumours of an incident involving General Franco at the golf club on the very day the other passenger was supposed to be playing golf.

More conflicting rumours, which were never confirmed, suggested that the General had held a high level meeting with other military commanders and civilians behind closed doors at El Peñon. During the meeting it was revealed that Franco would be departing immediately for Las Palmas to attend the funeral of another general, Amado Balmes, who had been shot in the stomach in mysterious circumstances. In fact it is believed the future dictator used that as an excuse to go to Las Palmas in order to board the de Havilland Dragon Rapide which was to fly him to Morocco for the start of the coup. The meeting at the golf club had been ordered to put the final regional touches to the conspiracy. It had been interrupted briefly by a noisy episode involving a foreign gentleman suspected of being a spy. The official word was that they believed, quite wrongly, that the man had been acting on behalf of the Republicans. In fact, if he was the same Spanish looking gentleman with the English name and the brown leather over-night bag, he had most probably been sent to keep a very close eye on proceedings by British Intelligence. How he was found out, if indeed he was, nobody will ever know. He may well have made an error. It might have been sheer bad luck. Everyone was on edge and anyone in the wrong place at the wrong time was immediately suspected of belonging to the other side. He would have been detained, taken away for cruel questioning and possibly shot.

The Spanish Civil War began on the very next afternoon when the military revolt was proclaimed in Africa. Rumours that the conspiring generals were about to be arrested had forced them to act in haste.

General Franco, awaiting news in Las Palmas, was awakened in the early hours of the 18th July. He was told the uprising had been a success and that the North African colony barracks at Tetuán, Ceuta and Melilla were his. He immediately put his wife and daughter on a ship bound for France before stepping onto the Dragon Rapide which took him to North Africa to lead the right wing revolt.

LEGS IN THE ORCHARD

Ruth Eastleigh was a relatively young lady in her early thirties when she decided to be adventurous, as certain contemporaries of hers were in the early 20th century. In her hometown of Lyme Regis she was considered quite an attractive girl, but no man had ever been able to distract her from her interests in nature, monuments and watercolours.

Having read so much about the islands in the Du Cane sisters' beautifully illustrated book about the Canaries, she arrived in Tenerife in 1926, entirely on her own, looking for tranquil adventure and the colours expressed by Ella Du Cane in her paintings. Perhaps she also sought to get as far away as she could from a wretched man who simply wouldn't take a hint. Well, that is what gossiping neighbours liked to imagine. However, the real problem with gentlemen was somewhere in Ruth's head. It was one that had tormented her for almost ten years and therefore greatly prejudiced her self esteem during those tender, ripening years. Ruth was deeply ashamed of her legs. They betrayed a not uncommon varicose vein problem. It was an unnecessary shame and therefore it is distressing to imagine how someone who in fact possessed strong and reasonably attractive legs could have seen her personal life hampered by what might today not seem to be such a nightmare.

Ruth planned to stay in Puerto de la Cruz for a number of weeks but she had been advised to break the journey in the agricultural town of Tacoronte. The road to the Orotava Valley was so tediously long and winding. So she took a simple, airy room at the Camacho Hotel with a pretty view towards the hills. The variety of colour in the sloping countryside, which she looked out upon from her balcony, filled Ruth with artistic inspiration and she hired one of the horses the hotel made available to guests for eleven and a half pesetas a day. The manager also offered to send Domingo as a guide. Ruth Eastleigh was hesitant to begin with. She was very much an English lady and not at all certain about the proposal. Nevertheless the manager assured her that the man who kept the hotel's garden so beautifully was entirely harmless. Domingo, he explained with a crooked grin, was not the slightest bit interested in women. Had Ruth not been afflicted by her modesty and embarrassment she might well have been disappointed. Domingo turned out to be a strong, tall and extremely handsome young man.

A bridle path led them to La Fuente de Agua García, a spring after which the area is named. It was a perfect spot to unsaddle and view the surroundings, and the island of La Palma's two humps peeped like well-formed breasts above the clouds on the distant horizon.

Ruth and her guide settled the horses into a small patch of lush grass just below a dense wood of willow, pine, and laurel. She took a deep breath, absorbing the scents coming from below, where there were cork and wild orange trees. Other fields on the slopes were dotted with palms and the hedgerows were a mixture of blackberries, bracken and a variety of ferns. Ruth might well have been somewhere in the English countryside. The air was bracing enough. But those brambles growing against neat stone walls seemed to produce a fruit that was even more delicious. She noticed how much the big green and blue lizards enjoyed the blackberries too, and wondered if the warmth of the black, volcanic stone had anything to do with their development and sweetness.

Whilst Domingo lay under a huge pine tree at a discrete distance, Ruth Eastleigh decided to sit on a rock overlooking a wild apple orchard on the other side of one of those stone walls she had peeped over. There were about a dozen women filling large sacks with generous, rough-skinned brown apples. She had been attracted by their singing and happy laughter. Most wore green, brown and cream coloured garments. Their heads were covered with bright scarves and large straw hats tied down with ribbons. A couple of the women were in black as a sign of strict mourning for a dead husband. Small children ran around half-naked and healthily dirty from playing in the red earth. One of Ruth's happiest memories of Tenerife was the jovial nature of ordinary folk working together in the crops as if they had not a care in the world in spite of their poverty.

Always aware of people's legs, when some of the women lifted up their dresses to gather apples in them before rolling the fruit into brown sacks and baskets, Ruth noticed that they all wore stockings up to just below their knees. She discovered later that the main reason for this was not so much in keeping with the fashion of the day but to protect their legs from the viciously biting flies which got under their long skirts as they worked in the fields.

Not long after she had begun sketching the

colourful scene one of the women, whom she later described in her diaries as peasant folk, clambered up onto her rock, sat down on the grass beside her, offered her an apple and smiled generously. In return Ruth offered the woman water from her pewter cup and an equally welcoming smile. It was accepted with gratitude. The rough-skinned apple was crisp, incredibly juicy and had a distinctive flavour which Ruth would never forget. After taking a sip of the water the woman rolled down her stockings, dampened her scarf in the water and dabbed it on her legs. To Miss Eastleigh's astonishment the peasant's legs were a web of varicose veins. They made hers look quite insignificant and yet the woman must have been of Ruth's age or perhaps slightly younger. Comforted by the sight and after a few moments of smiles and sign language the English lady lifted up her petticoat, pointed at her purple-blue veins and tried to express that they had something in common.

"Ouch! Sometimes very sore!" explained Ruth in an effort to share her own similar curse with the local field worker.

"*Bueno! Pero eso no es nada, señora.* But that's nothing!" replied the local woman, mocking the triviality of the foreigner's problem but understanding the good intentions and feeling very honoured indeed. She then shouted down at the others. To Ruth Eastleigh's amazement seven of the women stopped collecting apples, ran up to just below the rock, put one leg forward and rolled down a stocking to reveal that they too were afflicted with abominable varicosities. They then shrieked with laughter and ran back to their work.

Two months later, on her homeward passage to England on one of the Royal Mail Line steamers to Southampton, Ruth Eastleigh met the man of her life. He was the ship's young purser, a quiet fellow called Alan Bainbridge who happened to come from a town called Abbotsbury, just along the coast from Lyme Regis. They were married as soon as they could because of Alan's sea duties but also because they both longed for each other. Many years later, after the war which Alan survived despite twice being torpedoed by German U-Boats, there was still no doubt in Ruth's mind that the encounter with the peasant woman in the hills above a town called Tacoronte had changed her life. If the woman had not rolled down her stockings Ruth might always have remained at the mercy of her shame. She had shared an afternoon with a very happy group of Canary Island women, all young mothers who sang and laughed in the fields without a thought for varicose veins much more frightful than her own. That experience had been more helpful by far than a visit to a modern psychiatrist.

What is more, during her stay in Puerto de la Cruz, Ruth Eastleigh's shyness was overcome by immense joy and a growing confidence, especially after discovering that varicose veins were not only very common in this part of the world but also curable with a range of practical treatments. The varicose vein is commonly thought to be caused, amongst other things, by poor blood circulation, and the veins swell up exaggeratedly under pressure. Those tight stockings used by the apple pickers to keep the flies off were possibly one of the main causes for their high percentage of sufferers.

The kind lady who owned the Marquesa Hotel in Puerto de la Cruz provided Ruth with a daily bucket of cool water to which she added a handful of sea salt and vinegar. The English lady found this a great relief for her tired legs after a day's excursion. However she also felt the same relief when paddling in the rock pools at San Telmo, much to the delight of local men.

Ruth also discovered a number of strange and sworn-by remedies for the varicose vein. The gravedigger in one of the northern towns suffered from them. He always blamed the number of dead he had had to bury over the years. His wife, they said, rubbed his legs with a potion of olive oil mixed with crushed cypress corns, rosemary and garlic. Old wives and grandmothers used to tell expecting descendants to drink quantities of soup made with garlic, onions and leeks. Actually Ruth Eastleigh tried this particular soup and found it so delicious that one must assume her ship's purser had to learn to enjoy it on many a frosty English night. It has also been written about that a fisherman on the island of El Hierro rid himself completely of his varicose veins by drinking pineapple juice daily over a period of two years. Mind you he is also believed to have given up rum, fried food and hard cheeses, so one can only assume that his varicose veins must have been making his life unbearable.

A local remedy Ruth Eastleigh thought highly amusing, which also possibly gave her the privilege of being able to laugh at herself, is still very popular in some parts of the islands. It is quite harmless and does not involve eating things one does not like. The solution is to have a good swim in the cool sea and then to do hand stands or to stick ones legs up in the air against a wall for more than fifteen minutes, ignoring comments from passers-by. Being the skirted lady she was and never failed to be, Ruth was never quite tempted to try the remedy. Nevertheless it would have pleased all of the friends she made in Tenerife to know that it was here, on their island, that she discovered self-confidence and freed her mind of the inhibitions caused by her varicose veins.

A MYSTERIOUS UNCLE

Valle Gran Rey, on the Canary island of La Gomera, was still charmingly behind the times in the early 1970s. There was a unique quietness broken only by water gurgling down the irrigation channels or by the postman hooting the horn of his Morris Minor van. He came once a week from the capital, San Sebastian, and picked up eggs on the way in the town of Valle Hermoso. There was only excitement when the fishermen returned with their boats full of tuna and when their womenfolk helped shove their small laden craft onto the beach before the new harbour was built. The only foreign visitors were either the young Germans or the occasional British hippie. There were, of course, one or two learned *extranjeros*, foreigners who had been clever enough to take up permanent residence.

One of these was Mr. Nicolson, a quiet Englishman. From the very day he arrived and bought the *finca* around the cliff from the fishing village, local people in Valle Gran Rey had been generally impressed by his courteous manner. He kept to himself and that was appreciated. He was in his fifties and solitary. Villagers assumed he was very rich by his dignified walk and by the car he drove. The petrol station in Valle Gran Rey still had a hand pump in those days. The very first time the Englishman took his thirsty Range Rover to be filled up the attendant got so tired of pumping that he kept looking under the vehicle, swearing about his mother's milk. He was quite certain there must have been a leak in the petrol tank.

Mr. Nicolson spent the early mornings gazing out to sea like a sailor without a ship before sitting at his desk for most of the day clattering away at an ancient type writer.

Once in a while he would leave for a month or two in England, to attend to business, as he always told the housekeeper, Leonor. He employed her and almost every member of her family to look after the house, the garden and the banana plantation he had bought with the land.

When he returned after one of his more prolonged trips, three or four years after moving to La Gomera, he was accompanied by a young lad of about sixteen. It was his nephew, Sam. The boy had been expelled from one or two public schools and his parents simply didn't know what to do with him anymore. Instead of accepting an offer to send him cotton-picking at a friend's farm in Rhodesia, they packed him off with his kind uncle to learn about bananas in the Canaries. The boy's mother was concerned about the increase in terrorist activity against the white population in the old colony. She persuaded her husband that Sam required a gentler sort of education to bring out the best in him, and not a tough Rhodesian experience.

Actually Sam was very like his uncle and they got on perfectly. Mr. Nicolson had always been fond of his nephew. In fact he thought highly of him in spite of his record. He recognised an untapped intelligence and noble nature and realised that all Sam really needed was time to develop his self confidence. All the problems back home were merely a call for attention and possibly the result of a distant father, whose entire life centred on the stock markets and not upon helping to ease the boy into maturity. Mr. Nicolson soon began to send Sam off to Hermigua and other banana growing regions on errands with Manolo the lorry driver, or to help the men cut down and wrap the bunches of green bananas in blankets before dividing them and packing them up, ready for shipment.

It was at Hermigua, where a doctor friend called Mendez had invited the Englishman and his nephew to spend a weekend at his villa above the rocky beach that Mr. Nicolson began to be referred to, with some considerable respect, as that mysterious Englishman from Valle Gran Rey.

It all started when Sam decided to go for a swim at what the locals call *el peñon*. This is a natural inlet under the steep cliffs created by a flow of molten lava meeting the pounding waves thousands of years ago. It still is a magnificent place to swim in today and there is an old seawater pool built beside it. But *el peñon*, a long, deep and narrow gully is blessed by the action of the waves that come in and go out, constantly filtering the crystal clear water and providing a natural habitat for a variety of fish and crustaceans. In fact it is a paradise for youngsters and amateur divers exploring the haven beneath the surface.

It was still early morning when Sam walked down the cement steps to the gully. There was not a soul to be seen or heard except for an old fisherman looking for crabs to use as bait. Close to him a solitary seagull perched on a rock pretending to look possessively into a salty pond whilst keeping an eye out for scraps. Nevertheless Sam almost turned into a volcanic rock himself when he spotted what he would later describe as his mermaid. She was not just swimming. She was diving, surfacing and playing with the water like a porpoise, as if she lived beneath the surface. Sam was hypnotized for an instant by an enchanting and enticing display of innocent yet seductive aquatic ballet.

When the girl slid out of the water and settled herself gracefully onto a neatly laid towel on the black rock, he realised she was the most beautiful creature he had ever set eyes upon. Sam, the shy rebel, was immediately struck by what could have been love, but was possibly an indomitable and natural desire to find a way into the girl's life just for a day.

Very soon, as if all his self confidence had miraculously ignited, he was beside the girl and they were talking, in broken English, about the book she was reading. It was Johnathan Livingston Seagull, by Richard Bach, and provided an eternity of deep and thoughtful conversation between the two young and tender hearts. Like the seagull, they too were beginning to learn to fly through the clouds of the modern world and toyed with rebelling against conformity. When Sam discovered that her name was Tatiana he knew that indeed he must have been in love. Hers was a name made for poets, or so his young head imagined. He tried his hardest to impress the girl during most of the morning, but it was hopeless, for she abandoned him to go for lunch with her family without telling him where she lived.

However, they met again on the following morning. The girl told Sam that she lived in Tenerife and often spent her summer holidays with her family in Hermigua. She was fifteen and as cautious as any well brought up young lady from the capital, Santa Cruz, would have been.

"I am staying with my uncle in Valle Gran Rey", he said in answer to her belated enquiry. But then, perfectly innocently, jokingly in fact, he added, "He is a British spy. He comes here to escape from the Russians!" Exactly why he said that he would never know, but it worked wonders.

"*Un espía*, like James Bond *zero zero siete*?" she shrieked.

The girl was impressed, so much so that she forgot all about her caution and philosophical reading when they next dove deep into the waters. Tatiana suddenly took a hungry interest in Sam's bony good looks and just one stolen kiss in the waves and the touch of the girl's shoulder against his when they lay side by side on the shore was enough to satisfy Sam's dreams for the rest of his stay on the island. But he would never know the heights to which his uncle's reputation would be elevated as a result of his brief encounter with the mermaid.

The Englishman in Valle Gran Rey almost became a living legend. Tatiana told all her friends confidentially that Sam's uncle was a secret agent. They all told their mothers about Mr. Nicolson and the mothers reported the news to the lady at the shop. Naturally she couldn't keep it from the postman with the Morris Minor and he informed everyone on his rounds that the Spanish authorities knew all about the British submarine that has been sending coded signals from out in the bay.

Even fishermen in Valle Gran Rey spoke of how they had nearly caught a periscope in their nets.

Leonor, the housekeeper and her family kept a discrete, proud, faithful and ignorant silence. In fact Mr. Nicolson was never ever troubled by such innocent, youthful rumours. When he died, not so very long ago, someone heard that he had in fact been a writer of novels and not a spy at all. Nevertheless legends sometimes refuse to become mere pieces of fictional literature and often survive undamaged by truths.

THE BOY WITH THE MOON ON HIS HEAD

It was a difficult ride without having a local guide to point out the better mule tracks through the forests, but Hugo Stratton was determined to reach San José de los Llanos before sunset. He had been told about the magnificent view of Mount Teide, lit up by the orange evening sun, to be found from the plains below the village and he wanted to add another angle to his collection of sketches of the great volcano.

With a horse borrowed from Rio Reid, the British Vice-Consul's son in Puerto de la Cruz, Stratton had already discovered remote villages in the hills. He had also spent many a solitary night under the stars since arriving on the island of Tenerife in November 1927. A doctor had recommended a winter on the island to recover from a lung complaint developed in the trenches at Ypres. That is where he had battled alongside Rio's older brother, Captain Noel Reid, whom he described in his diaries as a splendid chap, absolutely fearless and always the cheeriest soul alive. Hugo, who often recalled why his gallant friend was awarded the D.S.O. and Military Cross medals, had been equally adventurous and fearless in battle, although he never mentioned it. He was therefore not in the least concerned about losing his way in the mountains on a small island. He was much more anxious about having to pass through El Llano de los Hermanos, where it was said that seven travelling friars had once frozen to death. There was something about that image which stirred hideous memories of frozen corpses in the trenches on the battlefront.

But when he got to El Llano, just after reaching the heath and pines, he was so taken by a sight of eleven volcanoes in a line, including the Chinyero, the last to erupt in 1909, that he completely forgot about the ghosts of dead holy men.

He reached San José by late afternoon with plenty of time to spare and decided to set up his well-used olive green tent on a small, sloping plain just to the west of the village. This, he noticed, was a collection of no more than two dozen stone cottages. He was greeted by men and women returning to their homes after a day in the fields and was gazed at for what seemed an eternity by a group of half naked children who had certainly never seen a tent before.

Stratton had become accustomed to being stared at by children during his travels in the remote rural areas and always resorted to the same trick to break the ice. He collected about twenty smooth stones which he put in a pile close to the tent. Then, certain that he was the centre of attention, he lay down on the ground and began to see how many of the stones he could pile one on top of each other before they collapsed. It was an entertaining game he had learnt in the trenches. During those few grateful lulls between fighting and bombardments, soldiers always found some distraction to help them forget and to pass the time.

By his third attempt, his tiny audience were clapping and laughing and anxious to join in the fun, which they did until mothers shrieked that it was time for them to leave *el ingles* alone.

Everything went quiet with the last bird song. The only sound to be heard was that of the pines whispering with the breeze and the occasional scurry in the long grass. Even the Englishman's horse got the hint that it was time to steady its restless hooves. But all of a sudden, just as Stratton spotted a large owl swooping low overhead in the moonlight, a man shouted and began to run.

Instinctively, Stratton reached for the revolver he always carried in his saddle-bag and leapt out of the tent into the shadow of a stone wall. These islanders were good, friendly people, but there was never any harm in taking precautions.

The single shout was followed by yelling from all directions, then by women's chatter and finally by laughter. The Englishman smiled to himself and came out of the shadows and into the moonlight. He replaced his weapon in the saddle-bag, lit a small fire inside a circle of stones and brewed himself a mug of tea. He was not going to be allowed to rest so he filled his pipe and sat on a mossy tree trunk beside his tent listening and watching.

Within an hour, when Hugo Stratton had assumed that he and all the villagers would have been peacefully asleep, one of the tiny cottages, the one nearest to his field, had been lit up by a magnificent bonfire and was surrounded by what appeared to be every single member of the community.

One of the women was evidently delegating whilst others carried what looked like pots and baskets inside the stone wall which enclosed the cottage. The men, meanwhile, stood around the fire talking and drinking. A normally quiet village night high in the mountains had turned into a spontaneous fiesta. None of the villagers wanted to be left out and before long music accompanied the crackling fire.

Some started playing *timples*, traditional Canary Island stringed instruments which are very similar to the ukulele. Others joined in with home-made drums and percussion instruments. They sang folk songs and danced, many moving in and out of the doorway holding hands. A short while later Stratton stood up when he heard heavy footsteps approaching over the hard, dry earth.

The man had brought him a cup of red wine which he more or less ordered Stratton to drink with a mischievous smile on his face. The Englishman sipped the bitter burgundy liquid and felt it burn as he swallowed, but this was followed almost immediately by a warm and pleasing sensation deep inside. He didn't hesitate when the man beckoned him to follow. Outside the cottage someone took his cup and refilled it before ushering him under the thatched roof.

The cottage had just one room. It was where the young family cooked, ate and slept. The floor was nothing but the cool, hard-trodden earth. The stove was a stone shelf against the wall under the chimney. This was a structure made with earth and stone and it led to a hole in the thatch. There were four simple, wooden chairs, a few pinewood stools and part of an old tree trunk. These were sat on by elderly folk and women in a crowded circle around a bed. In contrast to the rest of the belongings the bed was remarkably sophisticated. Beside it on the ground was a beautifully carved wooden cradle. On it a simple grey and blue blanket and a tiny white pillow waited in anticipation. A young woman lay on the bed under a patchwork coverlet. Her face was contorted and she was letting out low cries. Another woman dabbed her forehead with a wet cloth.

"María, aquí está el inglés, here is the Englishman!", shouted another, introducing an uncomfortable Stratton. He was the innocent guest of honour at a peasant's birth ceremony and he realised upon leaving the room that he would have to partake in the party whether he wished to or not.

It was the custom, as he later found out, that births, especially in rural areas of the Canaries, were celebrated with dances, music, games and a great deal of wine and feasting. Sometimes they could last for days and the expectant mother would often organise and liven up her own party to make the duty of giving birth less painful. He was lucky on this occasion. María's labour was very short.

A few days later, amongst more privileged lowlanders, the Englishman would think back at the dignity of the smile that young woman managed to offer him in between her contractions. He would also remember his initial shock and disbelief at the ceremony and then his realisation that there was something very good and noble about the custom. It portrayed a sense of community that would one day almost disappear as country folk sought better fortune in the big towns.

Soon after midnight, Hugo Stratton joined the revellers in a great cheer outside the cottage after a plump woman interrupted the music with news that María had given birth. The celebration continued well into the early hours of the morning and one by one men and women were invited in to see the mother and the newly born child. Stratton felt most honoured that these villagers should have wanted to share such an occasion with him, a total stranger. In fact he would never forget this and other examples of Canary Islanders' generosity and uninhibited kindness. It was a beautiful child and María's was a precious smile, this time prolonged, for the Englishman.

The boy was asleep and oblivious to the customary pain, exhaustion and celebration. But a ray of moonlight, shaped like a quarter moon, peeped through a tiny hole in the thatch and touched the boy's head, as if to remind Hugo Stratton that he was blessed to have just taken part in something so very unique and sacred.

PELLETS AND PEBBLES

This is a brief account of two tales. One is set in the heart of Edinburgh in 1972. The other begins in 1903, overlooking a colourful street in the old Puerto de la Cruz, on the island of Tenerife. They are almost identical in spirit and both occurred in the month of December. What is most remarkable is that they involved different generations of one family.

Jenny, whose full name I would prefer not to disclose, was a very pretty nineteen year old. Her family home was a farm on the River Tweed close to Peebles, but like most of her friends she became independent as soon as she moved up to university and shared a small third floor flat in heart of Edinburgh. One day, on her own and tidying up just before returning to the farm for Christmas, she discovered a loose floorboard under a bookshelf. To her astonishment, when she lifted the suspect board she found a black, metal box hidden under it. Getting down on her knees, she lifted it out carefully as it was quite heavy. She opened the lid.

Inside were a pair of old cricket boots, a well used cricket ball, a schoolboy's cap and an air pistol with a tin full of lead pellets.

Having been brought up on a farm Jenny knew all about guns and was delighted. If the pistol didn't belong to anyone she would give it to her younger brother as a Christmas present.

The very next day the church bells were chiming magnificently and she had the windows wide open. It was a beautiful, crisp Sunday morning in Edinburgh and the castle embankment wore a promising coat of frost. Jenny had made herself a mug of coffee and was sitting by the window playing idly with her new toy when a very mischievous idea caught her imagination. As I said, she knew all about guns and was well aware that a pellet from an air pistol of that calibre would not even kill a small rabbit unless it was at very close range. Nor was it Edinburgh's pigeons she was thinking about. But if a pellet were to accidentally hit a person, on a trouser leg for example, it would sting and make the poor victim jump, but little else. She decided, therefore, that it would be tremendous fun if she could attract the attention of any handsome young man who might happen to be walking down her street by taking a pot shot at his backside.

This she did. Naturally she was a very good shot. By lunchtime she had attracted seven sweet young fellows, including one strapping eighteen year old lad wearing a kilt, up to her flat. She had no alternative but to invite them all to fish and chips from the takeaway on the corner. It was the one in the kilt, a public school boy supposedly out for Sunday lunch with an uncle, who had the decency to go out to purchase a considerable number of cans of beer. The consequence of this was that her little bit of fun got very out of hand and the young men began to take it in turns to take shots at those innocent pigeons on Edinburgh's grey window ledges. Miraculously no windows were smashed and all the pigeons survived the sniping. However someone did report a shooting incident to the police and there was soon a tall man in blue knocking on Jenny's door.

Unfortunately for him he was a very good looking young officer and Jenny had not the slightest trouble in melting at the sight of him. This caught him off guard momentarily and the expression on his face betrayed mild amusement. Overflowing with charm she welcomed him to her party, offering him the most delicious and inviting smile she could muster. Furthermore, when the officer regained his composure and asked who was responsible for the rotten deed of shooting at the pigeons, she put her hand up very innocently. Of course, judging by the scrum of young men smiling at him irreverently from behind the girl, he would not believe a word of it.

"All right then, I will ask the question only once. To which of you gentlemen does this weapon belong?" he insisted.

"It's mine!" replied Jenny again very honestly indeed this time, hoping the gorgeous policeman would arrest her.

"No, officer, it is in fact mine", fibbed one of her seven sweet guests, trying to get her out of trouble with a remarkably straight face and a slightly slurred speech.

"Oh, no it isn't. Actually, the weapon in question belongs to me" said another in a superior tone. The same story was told by the remaining five swaying young gentlemen, including the one with the kilt who appeared to have sipped more of a share of ale than anyone else. All the young men owned up and took the blame. So did Jenny once again, pleading to be handcuffed. The police officer had a choice. He could either arrest them all or give in to their charms. In fact he did what any decent, firm and well trained Edinburgh policeman would do in the circumstances. He confiscated the gun, took down all their names and addresses and bade them good day.

A couple of days before Christmas a rather good looking young man turned up at the farm on the Tweed and asked to speak to Jenny. It was her policeman. He had brought her a beautifully wrapped up Christmas gift, inside of which was her air pistol and the beginnings of a tender love affair that remains intact to this day. But that is where the second tale begins, and it was Jenny's grandmother, after Christmas lunch, who unfurled an amazing coincidence.

"Your great grandmother painted that", she said, pointing to a small and enchanting watercolour hanging by the clock in the hall. It was signed M.F.W. and had been painted in1903. It showed the white walls of a foreign town with a dark grey church tower in the background. There were a couple of tall palm trees beside the church and a burgundy bougainvillea cascaded over the walls. "She did it on a clear December day during a picnic in a field outside a town called La Orotava, in Tenerife."

"She spent two months on Tenerife in 1903 accompanying my Aunt Florence who travelled there to recover from pneumonia. Mama simply loved the island. She painted two or three more like this, but I've no idea where they ended up. Actually, although she only ever visited the Canary Islands once, they remained in her heart forever. You see, that is where she fell in love with your great grandfather James.

"As far as I can remember, and it was a very

long time ago that she told me the story, your great grandmother became a bit restless one afternoon and did something foolish but very typical of her. She had collected a basketful of small pebbles from a beach and decided to throw them one by one from the balcony of their little hotel into the street below. The idea was to attract the attention of dark, handsome young Spaniards as they walked by. It worked rather well because the hotel manager very soon told Aunt Florence that a young man wanted to invite her and her niece to a dance at the magnificent Grand Taoro Hotel, which was up on a hill overlooking La Orotava's port."

He was not a Spaniard at all but an equally handsome, dark haired young Scottish traveller called James. He had been struck hard on the head by one of the pebbles. When he glared up to encounter a wicked smile he decided to seek sweet revenge.

"That, my dear, is how your great grandparents met and fell in love, and if I am not mistaken your appetite has not been the same since your policeman knocked on the door day before yesterday!"

WHEN THE WATER FLOWS

When I was a boy there was a water channel at the bottom of the garden. I didn't know where the water came from but whenever it appeared, about once a week in the summer and more often during the winter, I rushed down to see how fast a twig or a leaf would take to get from the beginning of the channel to where it disappeared down into the first banana plantation. The water was precious then and is even more so today with high demand from an over populated island.

My children can't play the same games today. The channel has been replaced by a large plastic pipe, the banana plantations have been developed into luxury villas, and the water, which still flows down the pipe as frequently as it did then, goes to supply big tanks for watering hotel gardens, to fill swimming pools or to feed thirsty new housing estates.

When my father first brought my mother to the island of Tenerife in the early 1950s she was just as innocent about the water as I was when I was that little boy. I know because of how she described her first tutorial on the laws which governed local water supplies.

"She is innocent!" said an old man who was looking on with nothing better to do. She was so innocent that she actually glared at the men who were pointing accusingly in her direction.

"She's a foreigner!" contradicted one of the men working in the adjacent field. That was the kind of remark that greatly annoyed my mother. She was about to defend herself in the little Spanish she had learnt, but immediately thought better of it. Instead she decided to pretend to remain indifferent and concentrated on what she was doing again.

At that point the newly employed gardener, Basilio, arrived on the scene. By the expression on his face he was just as astonished at what my mother was doing and suddenly appeared to be on the verge of a nervous fit. My mother thought that perhaps his conscious nature was stricken at the sight of a woman watering the beginnings of a garden, especially as he should have started in the garden at least an hour earlier. My mother then imagined that she had offended that kind of pride which can often stick closer to a Spaniard than his own shadow. Then it crossed her mind that perhaps the gardener considered the torrent of sparkling water she had diverted into her garden from the channel which ran along the garden wall was too strong for the freshly laid earth, and it was her turn to be anxious.

Basilio, who was cross-eyed, went up to my mother and looked at her as straight as his squinting eyes would let him. His lips trembled with emotion. My mother looked back at him, wondering which of his eyes she should focus on. The gardener seemed to anticipate the problem by clapping a hand over one eye and then interrogated the woman of his employer.

"Why didn't *la señora* wait until after dark?" he hissed.

My innocent mother failed to see the logic behind the question, and told him that the plants were dying from lack of water and that they could not wait until after dark.

Basilio removed the hand from his eye, turned round, and faced the growing crowd of *finca* workers who were showing every sign of having a thoroughly amusing time at the expense of the gardener and the foreign woman.

He shrugged his shoulders and catapulted his lower lip outwards to indicate that he neither knew or cared about what my mother was doing. He then sat on one of the stone walls dividing the fields, crossed his legs, lit a cigarette and gazed back at her.

My mother was outraged. She would not stand for this impertinence. Nor did she like the feeling of being the object of amusement. Besides, she had spent a lot of time, energy and ingenuity damming the water in the channel with a portion of banana trunk. She had seen the men do this in the plantations when they irrigated the bananas. How dare the man she paid to look after the garden just look on while she did all the work?

The same old man who had earlier defended her ambled up to the edge of the garden.

"Perhaps you had better call your husband", he suggested. That is what my mother, who was quite sensible most of the time, decided he had said and she walked towards the house with as much dignity as she could.

"We must get Basilio a watch", she said, interrupting my father's accounts.

"Why?"

"He waters the zinnias and then comes to the back door to know the time. Then he rakes half the drive and asks the cook what time it is again. Then he forgets about raking the rest of the drive, weeds some of the rose beds and comes to ask if it is lunchtime yet. Listen darling, I'm trying to water the garden and I need your help".

"You're not carrying watering cans about when the buses go past, are you?"

That he should make that remark surprised my mother. It was the maids, always more watchful of proprieties than my mother, who had laid down the one unbreakable law that it was a *verguenza*, an embarrassment for the lady of the house to be seen performing manual labour in public, especially when the buses were going by.

"No. I'm doing much better than that. I've dammed the *atarjea* and the garden is flooding splendidly, but the gardener refuses to help!"

With the speed and sound of a cork leaving a champagne bottle, my father left his chair spinning and charged passed my mother like an enraged bull into the garden. When my mother followed more sedately she discovered a mass of hands being flung skyways in all directions. In front of my father every member of the banana plantation brigade were giving their own kind of logical explanations about the water flowing pleasantly into my mother's garden.

"It's the water of Don Salvador.......the *canalero* will be furious......someone has already informed......she is a foreigner......"

My father wrenched my mother's neatly cut lock-gate from the channel and threw it over his shoulder. The sparkling water resumed its interrupted course down the trough with a grateful wave. Basilio flicked his cigarette into the bananas while the crowd of workmen, with good-natured grins, dispersed to their labours in the fields.

"I suppose you know you've been stealing water", said my father sternly and with a hint of disbelief. "How long have you been doing this for? According to the men you've had at least half an hour's worth. The gardener will know from the water man when it is our turn to take water. You've been stealing some of Don Salvador's share for his bananas!"

"What do you mean, stealing? But this channel runs through our garden! Whose water is it?"

My mother suddenly felt a flush of shame filling her cheeks and her eyes looked in every direction. Why hadn't anyone told her? Why didn't the brave men try to explain that she was helping herself to someone else's water instead of looking on amusingly at the innocent foreign woman?

That flushing shame began to turn to outrage again when Basilio crept up to her like a beguiling cat. He placed a hand over his left eye and then changed to the right as if the eye he focused with depended upon what time of day it was. The uncovered eye swung round like a needle to the magnetic north and invited my mother to look into it.

"*Señora*, I told you to wait until it was dark. Then nobody would have been any wiser!"

That was the day my mother learned that water in the Canary Islands is as dramatic a commodity as gold is to governments. She discovered that it is constantly talked about. Its quality is compared, and shares in water galleries are highly sought after. In those days there were still parts of the island that were short of water or to which water for irrigation was still not channelled, so she soon realised what value it commanded among the islanders. Indeed she was to fall under the spell of *las aguas* herself one day. The water that flowed down the channel through the garden once or twice a week belonged to shareholders and tenants who kept strict and honest rules about channelling irrigation water off into their properties only when it was their turn to do so.

The distribution of irrigation water and timetables were and still are kept by the water men, known as *canaleros* or canal men. Strictly speaking, those who aren't plumbed in to the main town water network have to grab their share when the water flows. If it is flowing at night and one has to take one's share from two to four in the morning, one just has to get up and do so. Otherwise one misses ones quota of water. But, like most ordinary folk in Tenerife, the *canalero* is a reasonable man and tries to adapt the flows of water to suit individual needs. For example, large water tanks for agricultural irrigation can be filled during the night without a danger of overflowing, whereas small holders can usually be accommodated to take their share when it best suits them. In winter months the water man almost begs one to take water, even if it is a dribble, just so as to distribute it somewhere. It isn't as simple as turning a tap off deep inside the mountains where the waters come from. The reverse happens in the hot summer months when great quantities of water are needed for irrigation. That is when storage tanks get low and people become desperate for their share of water. They then remember to be polite to the *canalero*. But he will never let one run dry. He makes quite a profit out of his occupation. Besides, water is a sacred right.

THE SORE TOOTH

Just two sleepless nights and miserable days after arriving in Puerto de la Cruz in December 1947 young Reverend Charles Lowe could not stand it any longer. He decided that he should take God's advice without further delay and pay a terrifying visit to a dentist.

His hostess, Lisette, a distinguished member of the small British community in the Orotava Valley, had already noticed how very pale and uncharacteristically quiet he had become and decided to ask discretely if anything was the matter.

"I've a dreadful toothache and really don't think I will be very good company if I don't have something done about it immediately", he confessed.

Reverend Lowe, known as Charlie to his friends, was on his way back to England after spending the war in Salisbury as chaplain to the First Battalion of the Royal Rhodesia Regiment. Lisette's eldest son had been Charlie's commanding officer and he had accepted an invitation to spend Christmas in Tenerife before continuing the journey home.

"It actually began to trouble me aboard the Edinburgh Castle but I prayed it would simply disappear. Instead it has become considerably worse, I'm afraid".

The Edinburgh Castle was one of those magnificent Union Castle Line ships that once did the South, West and East African routes from Southampton. At least one of them used to call in at Tenerife or Las Palmas once a month until the 1960s. The company's head office was in London's

Fenchurch Street and their agents in Tenerife were Hamilton and Company in Santa Cruz. The Reverend dearly wished now that he had taken advantage of the ship's proper English dentist, dreading the thought of what he imagined might be primitive methods on an Atlantic island.

"You men are all the same, Charlie. A sore tooth does not just disappear. You had better go and see our friend Roberto at once. This damp weather will just make it worse and I cannot have a bad tempered preacher in my house". Lisette, a very beautiful and elegant lady, was a kind and charitable woman. But she would not suffer fools and was also known to be quite blunt when it was necessary.

"Who on earth is Roberto for goodness sake, and what the devil has the weather got to do with it?" exclaimed the chaplain, by no means a submissive man himself, but showing signs that a sore tooth was obviously stretching his saintly manner beyond reason.

The weather was not cold. In fact it was quite sticky for the time of year, but the *panza del burro*, the donkey's belly as local inhabitants call the cloud that so often hangs over the Orotava valley, was said to make certain people's teeth sensitive, much as rheumatic bones become in damp conditions.

Don Roberto was the first in a generation of a famous family of dentists. That very afternoon

Andrés, the chauffeur, was told to be ready at dawn for the long and twisting drive to La Laguna. That is where the dentist had his original surgery before moving to the capital, Santa Cruz. By early evening Reverend Charles Lowe began to feel as if he was somebody being prepared for a dawn execution. One has to understand that going to the best dentist in Tenerife in 1947 was not yet as common and recommended as it would be fifty years later. There was a man in Puerto de la Cruz but one only went to him to have an extraction and apparently after having gulped a number of glasses of whisky.

What was happening to Charlie was exceptional. So was the behaviour of the servants. In fact the occasion seemed to take over the entire household. There was certainly a high state of excitement and the Reverend's hostess was acting rather like his commanding officer. Consequently very few members of the estate actually had a good night's sleep. The only one to have a decent rest for a change was the good Reverend. That was entirely the fault of old María, the cook. She had brewed up a couple of potions for the Reverend's tooth. In the first place she made him take two cups of camomile tea. There was nothing unusual in that. But she did shout at José, the gardener, to pick some parsley. She crushed it up with a spoonful of olive oil. She then rolled up a ball of cotton wool, dipped it into the potion and persuaded Reverend Lowe to place it upon the malevolent tooth. After a while he could not tell whether it was the effect of this old cook's remedy or the continuous drip of whisky offered by Lisette which had done the trick, but he drifted into a deep and peaceful sleep.

He was awakened at the crack of dawn, even before the cocks began competing across the valley. This did not amuse him at all, and there was worse to come. Although the air temperature was still rather warm he was tucked into the hostess's limousine with rugs, pillows and a hot water bottle. He fumed with embarrassment, and his face reddened to dangerous levels. The most reverent gentleman was struggling to control a fearsome outburst. Nevertheless he had begun to understand these people and a knowing smile and a wink from Lisette persuaded him not to be such a bore. Instead he decided to feel amused and charmed by the tumultuous send-off he was given by all members of the household, including gardeners and servants. This was an example of Christianity and he was grateful. Indeed, he could feel a sermon taking shape.

When they reached La Laguna he was actually grateful for the rugs. There was a bitter wind blowing over the Anaga hills as he stepped from the car onto slippery cobbles outside the surgery.

At least a dozen other ashen-looking patients were already waiting to be seen by the dentist and the Reverend felt very uncomfortable when he was immediately taken in, apparently jumping the queue, after Andrés the chauffeur had presented his *señora*'s compliments. Nevertheless Reverend Charles Lowe was pleasantly surprised, especially when Don Roberto said he did not think it would be necessary to extract the tooth. Furthermore, in the absence of modern high-speed drills that one can hardly tolerate without a good dose of anaesthetic, this 1947 island dentist worked like a sculptor, very gently and with the skill of a maestro. He was thoughtful enough to provide a pain-numbing injection, which was usually only applied for extractions in those days. Then, with a treadle driven drill and what appeared to be a minute set of chisels, he began to excavate the decayed parts, before introducing some kind of disinfectant.

Don Roberto patted the Englishman on the shoulder, gave his nurse an order, opened double doors into garden and went out. To Charlie's amazement the dentist then proceeded to cut some roses and ferns before disappearing out of sight for some considerable time. Meanwhile, out of the corner of his eye a much relieved patient watched as a nurse heated copper pellets in a spoon over a Bunsen burner until they melted. She then screwed the content up in some gauze to remove the mercury which she collected in a tiny glass bottle. She weighed it and a precise amount of silver amalgam before mixing them together in a bowl.

When the gentle dentist returned, Charlie's filling was ready to be inserted. The beautifully adorned roses, Don Roberto said with great Spanish charm, were for the enchanting *señora* Lisette.

The population in these islands just after the Second World War was still relatively small. There could only have been about eight thousand souls in Puerto de la Cruz and eating habits were simpler. Indeed investigators have no doubt that simple living did help maintain good teeth and healthy mouths. Ordinary folk were quite happy with a diet of *gofio*, goat's cheese, hard bread and chestnut or vegetable soups. Fishermen and people living in coastal areas always seemed to have the best set of teeth. Some say it was because they spent more hours in the sun. Others suggest they had the good habit of cleaning their mouths and gargling with seawater. Really old wives remember using powdered vegetable carbon to clean teeth or to cure certain problems. But there is no doubt that the average modern man has forgotten or ignores the virtues of a good herb. In some remote areas older people will still be seen to chew on rosemary or on a willow leaf after meals. Indeed, from what they say, a good chew on herbs or an extended gargle with the juices of crushed thyme, rosemary, or elderberry leaves can do miracles for the teeth and gums.

The Reverend Charles Lowe spent a very

pleasant Christmas in Puerto de la Cruz and a day or two after visiting Don Roberto he became his usual, witty self. He was a most entertaining guest and other members of the small British community who had the pleasure of inviting him to dinner or to their magnificent tea parties considered him a breath of fresh air. It was whispered about, after being invited to give a sermon at All Saints Church, that one or two members of the congregation proposed he should replace the chaplain of the day. However they were a very loyal lot and his hilarious sermon soon drifted into people's memories.

Charlie developed a soft spot for María, the cook. He teased her at every opportunity and she spoiled him without mercy. A special glint in Charlie's eyes whenever he greeted her became quite noticeable and it was evident that María had placed him on a pedestal. On occasions her efforts to please the man of prayer appeared touched by some divine intervention.

She made absolutely certain that a bottle containing another magic potion was placed in his bathroom every evening, just to keep the devil away.

It became the third necessary ingredient to his after-dinner ritual and followed a glass of whisky and a prayer. Thus, trusting first in God and then in the Spanish cook, the Reverend never failed to gargle with her very bitter concoction of white horehound and basil.

THE TALE OF A SCOTTISH CANARY

In 1903, when Puerto de la Cruz was still known as Port Orotava, a young Scottish gentleman took a room with a balcony at the Marquesa Hotel. He spent the first three days recovering from a severe attack of sea sickness on his outward journey from Liverpool. Like most travellers in those days he had all the time in the world for his health to improve. After all, he was comfortably well off as far as travelling expenses were concerned and the Marquesa, situated as it is today opposite the main church, cost him only eight pesetas a night. Nevertheless, he was anxious to discover Tenerife, especially Mount Teide. The great volcano greeted him every morning when he stepped out onto the balcony.

The Marquesa, one of the first magnificent town mansions to be turned into a hotel, was much frequented by British travellers and he very soon learnt that Doña Juana, the proprietor, could get the doorman to introduce him to the man who kept horses for hire. The Scot may not have been a good sailor but he was an excellent horseman and well accustomed to spending long periods camping out on his own exploring the border regions of Scotland for a barn or an old bridge to sketch. As soon as he felt strong enough he packed provisions for three days and went to the stables where he had already chosen a horse. It cost him thirty five pesetas for the week.

With his old tent rolled up behind him and saddle bags bulging, he mounted a placid mare the stable boy called Rubia. She was a pretty chestnut with a dainty, blond mane, but he had carefully chosen her for strength and character.

He rode out of the port, courteously raising the brim of his hat to everyone he met in reply to their *adios amigo*. Following a suggested route and an old map given to him the previous evening by a young English resident whom he had met at the English Library, he headed eastwards and up the hill past the botanical gardens, which he reached in no more than twenty minutes. Just above the gardens he then joined a stone track which climbed in an almost straight line towards the town of La Orotava. He passed men leading fully laden mules and donkeys, some carrying fruit or potatoes and others with strapped down firewood or demijohns with wine for the taverns. Women towing infants and carrying colourful bundles on their heads greeted him with cheerful whoops and smiles. This was the old road which connected La Orotava with its busy trading port. At a huge fallen rock which was well marked on the map he took one of the two suggested tracks. He walked the horse down into a *barranco* and up the same ravine for a few minutes until he came to a farmhouse on the right. He was able to mount again as the ground became even and rode slowly up a narrow path beside the ravine until he reached the road that led from La Orotava to the village of La Perdoma.

Like almost every road in those days it was a simple, dusty carriage track hardened by a lack of rain. After heading westward for a short distance, meeting more heavily laden mules and oxen carts, he turned left into yet another ravine. In normally wet February conditions this would have been slippery and dangerous. But there had been little rain since October and his horse made good progress up the hillside, through fields, around small woods and past tiny, thatched stone cottages where half clothed peasant children ran to meet him and to beg something in return for a smile.

Rubia found the climb easy. The Scotsman sensed that she had been there many times before. She seemed to know her way around and he almost let her lead him towards Mount Teide and his next reference point, a giant solitary pine. However, just below La Fuente de La Cruz, one of the many springs where local people collected drinking water and where women washed their linen, the mare appeared to develop a problem and became lame. Dismounting, he inspected each hoof for damage, found nothing apparently wrong and led the animal as far as the spring.

But Rubia's trouble persisted and she limped painfully, finding difficulty putting down one hoof. Thinking it might have something to do with a fetlock joint he walked her into the pool of icy water under the spring, hoping it might soothe her. When she had drunk and was satisfied he hung the reins loosely over some scrubs where there was some lush grass for the mare to chew.

The spring, hidden under an overhanging rock in another small gully, was at 3,000 feet above sea level and the air was much cooler. However both the horse and the Scot were steaming after the climb. He put his head under the gushing water which had been channelled along a piece of bark and sat down to decide what to do next. Rubia appeared to be limping less but he could not risk riding a lame horse all the way to Mount Teide. That expedition would have to wait.

He looked around him and smiled. What a wonderful place to be in splendid solitude, and what a dream of a sketch he could do. With the distant sea in the background, an old chestnut tree was half enclosed by a crumbling stone wall and surrounded by a covering of magnificent violets.

He sketched for over an hour. The mid-day sun began to peep through with a winter sting and as the Scot became more enthusiastic with his work of art so did his need to cool down. He was soon wearing nothing more than a pair of rolled up flannel trousers.

He had wandered so deeply into thought that the silence of the hills and the icy running water were all he could hear as he splashed his face under the spring and bathed his feet in the pool one more time. This time, when he turned around again to continue sketching he nearly fell backwards into the pool. Gentle Rubia was not the only living creature gazing back at him. He was being stared at by half a dozen women with water pots upon their heads, and there were four or five young girls hanging on to their aprons. All the women, except for one who was tall compared to the others and stood slightly apart, wore colourful dresses and headscarves. The tall one was dressed almost entirely in Russian blue garments. Her long reddish hair was loose and wild, and she wore a yellow scarf around her neck. Like the other women her feet were bare but she had not come to collect water. The pale stranger in the pool with the rolled up flannel trousers and the dripping hair noticed her step back to sit on a rock, and she looked on with an amused expression on her face as if anticipating the start of a French comedy.

After a moment of mild embarrassment the Scot realised that he must have provided an interesting sight to these gentle island folk. They can't have been accustomed to finding an evidently eccentric foreigner at their watering hole, especially with so little clothing on. So he could think of nothing better to do than to accept his predicament, grin embarrassingly and shrug his shoulders. The reaction was miraculous and unanimous. Every one of the country ladies said *buenos dias inglés* and shrieked with laughter for several minutes.

The Scot, who soon regained most of his composure and began buttoning up his shirt, returned the compliments but added that he was not an Englishman.

"Escocés", he said. "I am from Scotland".

That didn't make the slightest difference to the local women. As far as they were concerned he was still *inglés*. That would make an interesting psychological study. Even then, at the height of the British Empire and amongst the fortunate social classes, there seemed to be an urgent need for a man to explain to an innocent gathering of illiterate peasant women that there was a vital importance in not calling a Scot an Englishman.

However, he was still a gentleman and became supremely courteous and accepted the momentary friendship of these humble women. In fact he was fortunate to have shown such good manners and charm so soon after apparently looking so foolish. The tall young woman with the wild hair had stirred something deep inside him. Not only did she dress differently. She also had the most stunning green eyes which seemed to penetrate to the very depths of him. She was clearly not like the other women with their pots. Her stance was proud and arrogant and she was suddenly the most attractive and sensual woman he had ever set eyes upon.

She too appeared to have found something profoundly interesting in him because she lifted her long blue dress and petticoat up to her knees and skipped across the pool of water. She stroked Rubia's neck and rubbed her cheek against the horse's neck as if it were a long lost friend. Then she turned round, smiled enticingly and inspected the eccentric young Scotsman's art. The woman with the reddish wild hair said she liked his sketch of the violets, the chestnut tree and the sea in the background and then introduced herself. To his amazement she spoke the most perfect English.

She didn't leave him when the other women collected their water and made their way back down the hill. Instead she sat down on the grass and in the violets, and the two strangers began to know each other. By late afternoon they had fallen passionately in love.

The lady at the watering hole was the daughter of an aristocrat in La Orotava. However, unlike other members of her class, she enjoyed nothing more than to share the freedom and uninhibited laughter of the women and men who worked on her father's land. There were plans, on account of her rebellious nature, to send her to a convent in Seville the following year.

The young Scottish gentleman returned to Melrose to spend a rather long, impatient summer at his family home. He had some considerable explaining to do to his father and mother about why he needed to withdraw further funds in order to return to the island of Tenerife. He arrived back in the Orotava Valley in the early autumn just in time to witness the birth of his son. His lady with the wild hair was a disgrace to her family and was practically disowned. The Scottish gentleman bought her a small cottage just outside the port. There they lived happily ever after until an inherent sense of duty made him take the first ship home to fight and die for his country in 1914.

A year or two later the lady of the watering hole agreed to marry another British resident. He was the same Englishman at the English Library who had given her lover the old bridle path map to the mountains.

Her son grew tall and strong. The boy had his

father's blonde curls and his mother's green eyes. Everyone knew him as *el escocés canario*, the Scottish Canary.

TIRED FEET

Noel Reid watched as the old Spantax Airlines Douglas Dakota DC-3 lifted its tail and then appeared to hop along the runway at Los Rodeos airport before making one last effort with a glorious old-fashioned roar. It was the early 1960s and he was meeting his sixteen year old daughter. She was due back for the Easter holidays from her school for young ladies in Devon.

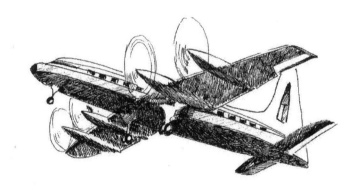

Right on schedule he then spotted the rather larger outline of the whispering giant from England. She was a British United Airways Bristol Britannia aircraft sparkling on the horizon before making her final approach over Santa Cruz.

His teenage daughter was very excited. She had met a group of university geology students on the flight and had evidently had a wonderful time conquering their hearts. The young men from Cardiff University were on a two-week field trip to Tenerife in order to study the island's volcanic rock formations. She had oozed charm and promised the lads that her family, which ran the Vice-Consulate in Puerto de la Cruz, could help them in any way they wished. Her father was grateful that she had not gone as far as to invite them all to stay at home, something she was quite capable of doing without prior notice. There were seven of them. In fact they were well equipped with tents and had a well documented and planned route. Their first stop was at Guimar, on the south east of Tenerife and they were to make their way over the hills to the base of Mount Teide before descending down, via the town of La Orotava, to spend their final two days enjoying a break by the sea in Puerto.

A rather odd looking gentleman with a Leyland Commer mini-bus was at the airport to meet the students. He was the brother of the man who was to be their guide. Before they parted company the students promised to look in on the Reid daughter as soon as they got to Puerto.

The young geologists were eager to get started early the next day and began to climb upwards through the valley from the scattered town of Guimar. It was a thriving farming community of about ten thousand inhabitants. A number of them put down hoes and baskets and greeted the foreigners as they strode upwards in single file on the narrow tracks which divided the fields.

Their first camp was in the wild and precipitous Barranco de Badajos. This was a deep and spectacular ravine inside of which they set out to explore the Cueva del Cañizo, a stone-age cave dwelling. When the Spanish conquerors arrived in the fifteenth century it was inhabited by aboriginal Guanches. The students were impressed by the ravine's natural beauty but found the cave somewhat disappointing. It was neither as deep nor ghostly as they had hoped. In fact it stank of goats and there was evidence that it was home to a large herd. As most of Guimar's water came from deposits deep within the ravine, the steep black walls were luxuriant with vegetation including an extraordinary variety of plants and ferns. The main water gallery, which was close to the top of the ravine, was called La Madre del Agua, the Mother of Water.

But the geologists had chosen the valley of Guimar as a first site for their investigations because they wanted to explore the incredible Garganta de Guimar, a narrow gorge through which the valley of Guimar meets the Orotava Valley on the north side of the island. In order to reach the depths of the gorge the Cardiff students needed to make a steep three-hour climb through the Monte Verde forest and across a remarkable expanse of black sand.

Laden with camping gear, instruments and provisions this was not an easy task, but the breathtaking scenery and regular sips of cool water lessened the burden. Towards the entrance of the gorge they were stunned by what must be one of the most stupendous efforts of eruptive force to be seen in the world. The students later described in their notes how the base of the gorge was covered by volcanic ash and by the detritus of the neighbouring rocks. The sides, about five to seven hundred feet in height, had not been affected by the action of water and were divided by an extraordinary system of dykes. The gorge had been created by an enormous force of secondary eruptive explosions that pierced through the walls of Las Cañadas, the island's original giant crater. These had permitted the flow, not only of molten lava into the valley of Guimar, but of water from subterranean deposits.

The seven lads from Cardiff were keen and well prepared with instrumentation and warm clothes to cope with the sudden changes in temperature at this height, but they had not been prepared for walking and climbing on so many different kinds of terrain. Consequently many of them very soon suffered twisted ankles, horrible blisters and very tired legs. Progress became slower than planned and certainly less enthusiastic. Nevertheless they had a mission and were determined to investigate as much as they could during the coming days. Manolo, their local guide, was no doctor, but he tried to help them. In fact he was more of a philosopher and an amateur naturalist and frequently told the students off for their modern ways.

"You English", he said, "have lost contact with the mother earth. You depend too much on leather shoes. You ignore the healthy sensation of stepping barefoot on the cool grass, on walking through mud and upon stones. It is only when you go to the beach with your girls that you discard your shoes and let your feet breathe".

Manolo was no doubt correct in his assertion. Even in our more advanced days, forty years on, it is admitted openly that tight shoes, high heels and sticky socks stop our feet breathing and it is wise to stroll about barefooted as much as possible in the fields, in the garden and on the beaches. Manolo, who took his responsibility as guide very seriously, almost ordered the lads to take his advice and before long had them removing their footwear at every opportunity, letting their pale and often very smelly soles breathe in the delicately scented and fresh mountain air. Whenever they could they dangled their tired and painful feet into *atarjeas*, the man-made channels that brought water from volcanic reservoirs deep inside the mountains. Some waters were icy cold. Others appeared to be warm and steamed a reminder that volcanic turmoil still existed within the island's heart.

Their geological investigations were nevertheless completed satisfactorily and they began their descent from the planetary landscapes of Las Cañadas feeling quite proud of their accomplishment. But it was as they began to descend the northern slopes that their poor feet and legs began to suffer most and some of the students even found themselves walking backwards so as to relieve tightening calf muscles.

At Aguamansa they took the decision to rest for a day. It was here that they discovered the real Canary Islander, the kind of people the islands were renowned for amongst early foreign travellers. The boys received exceptionally kind attention from local peasants whose lives were spent working in the fields. One man brought a basket of freshly cut sage and black vines. He came with instructions from his formidable wife that the strangers should crush the two herbs together, boil them up and then bathe their feet in the resultant tea. The object of this was in fact to soothe sweaty and odorous feet. Another much kinder lady, dressed all in black due to the loss of a husband, offered lavender flowers and rosemary for them to place inside their socks. Like the herb, her name was Rosa María. The students took to her immediately for she was not an old widow. She was young and attractive.

She thought nothing of washing the young men's feet for them, which gave them a perfect opportunity to peep down between her small, perfectly rounded breasts. They eagerly took their turns before filling their hungry stomachs with the most delicious water cress soup she made for them. As was the way, local people were always cordial and never suspicious of strangers, especially if they were as polite and respectful as these well educated British students.

By the time they reached Puerto de la Cruz and set up their tents, some on the Reid's lawn and others in the nearby garden of their good friend, Mr.

Ray Baillon, the young geologist's foot problems had disappeared. In fact all of their feet were also remarkably smooth and well scented. Sitting around the evening fire in Aguamansa they had learnt a few tricks. There was nothing better for tired legs than a good rub with boiled aromatic herbs and olive oil. If, on the other hand, the discomfort was caused by cold feet or by cramp, an old fellow who had spent a lifetime ploughing fields with oxen suggested bathing the legs in a potion produced by boiling mustard leaves, black peppers and onions. The wise old man warned them that they should then immediately wrap up the feet in a towel and go to bed. Not one of the students admitted to suffering from cold feet.

The lesson they learnt best of all, especially from Rosa María, the pretty young widow of Aguamansa, was that feet hygiene should be taken just as seriously as the hands. She could not understand why their English mothers had not packed them off with more than two pairs of socks and scolded them with an alluring smile for not washing their feet more frequently. Her reprimands only intensified the love and longing in the eyes of one or two of the young geology students from Cardiff.

NEW YEAR ON PIAZZI'S MOUNTAIN

With long telescopes objects can appear to be more brilliant and larger than with short ones, but even so they cannot be calibrated to eliminate the confusion of rays caused by the trembling of the atmosphere. The only remedy is to find a quiet and still place, like one at the top of the highest mountains, from which to make astronomical observations.

That is an apparently primitive opinion, if we take into account the telescopic material available to scientists today, but it was what Sir Isaac Newton suggested to his contemporary astronomers in 1730. It is also the advice another British astronomer, Charles Piazzi Smyth, took in 1856 when he set up camp close to the summit of Mount Teide. His experiments in Tenerife, of which local historians have written about with considerable pride, and his use of photographic equipment, were what transformed him from the virtually unknown son of a British admiral into an acclaimed international scientist, and Astronomer Royal of Scotland.

He was greatly assisted by Robert Stephenson, the famous engineer, who loaned Smyth his splendid steel-hulled yacht, the *Titania* and its crew. Stephenson was very generous and assured his fellow scientist that he could make use of her for the journey from Southampton to Tenerife and for however long it took to complete his investigations on the island.

The Titania sailed at a maximum speed of ten knots and arrived at Santa Cruz on the morning of 8th July.

Work began almost immediately to unload the complex and fragile scientific cargo which had been packed in wooden crates. Some of these had to be carefully dismantled prior to loading instruments and provisions onto horses and mules before sunrise on the following morning. A crowd of inquisitive onlookers, including the British Consul, the Mayor and other dignitaries gathered to watch the scientist's convoy of twenty seven animals and even more local porters make its way out of the port for the long trek up into the hills. Charles Piazzi Smyth, who had taken the advice of a resident mathematician, decided that the summit of Mount Guajara, at nearly 9,000 feet, the highest after Mount Teide, would be an ideal location from which to make his observations. It was a hard and steep climb.

The sun was setting when the party reached the summit on the eve of the second day. It would soon be dark and a number of the local carriers were not volunteering to spend an uncomfortable night breathing in the dry, choking air and sleeping in the open on hard, rocky ground. Consequently, without awaiting further orders, many just vanished very rapidly down the hillside as soon as they had unloaded the animals. Shelters had been prepared for them in the Valley of Ucanca where the soft pumice made more comfortable bedding and where a spring offered a welcome trickle of water. Jessie, Charles Piazzi Smyth's wife, to whom credit was given rather belatedly for her photographic material, observed in her diaries that the situation seemed desperate to begin with when some of the porters abandoned them, but that as soon as they had the tents up and sipped a warm cup of tea they all felt much better. In fact the men down in Ucanca had to work more they anticipated. The expedition was forced to move a few days later to Alta Vista, high on Mount Teide, because a constant haze of dust encountered from Guajara interfered with Piazzi's experiments. Conditions for the porters who accompanied the expedition on the great volcano were even harder but they were described as good natured workers with admirable physical strength.

Charles Piazzi Smyth had borrowed two of the Titania's crew, the ship's carpenter and a very enthusiastic young officer. They were both very co-operative throughout. Another young member of the crew, Jamie Burrows, had also volunteered but was disappointed at the last minute. The Captain required him on board during the first days of the expedition.

Nevertheless Burrows returned to Tenerife in December 1862 with his wife Ruth, not as a member of the Titania's crew but as part of their six-month honeymoon travelling across Europe. They were both adventurous young people, especially Ruth who later took part in ethnographic investigations for the British Museum, and their intention was to spend at least one month exploring some of the Canary Islands. Jamie was determined to visit that spot at the top of Mt. Guajara. His colleagues had described the great mound enthusiastically, especially the magnificent view towards Mount Teide and down into Las Cañadas, one of the world's largest and most breathtaking volcanic craters.

What Burrows didn't know was that Charles and Jessie Piazzi Smyth had also been on their honeymoon when they came to the island to carry out their observations on Guajara.

Jamie and Ruth used an English guesthouse in Port Orotava as a base and shared what Ruth would later recall as a solemn, Presbyterian Christmas with members of the small British community in the Orotava Valley. Nevertheless, they were treated with courtesy. Many very kindly offered assistance, except with their idea of going into the hills in mid-winter. They considered that idea very foolish indeed.

The young people refused the loan of a guide but did borrow two splendid horses from a Spanish aristocrat in La Paz who had himself spent a number of nights on Mount Teide reporting on Piazzi Smyth's 1856 expedition for a local newspaper. He was a great admirer of brave and eccentric British scientists. Burrows and his wife rode up into the hills against everyone's advice. As it so often is in late December, the weather was beautifully sunny and clear, so they saw no reason for all the concern.

It was still magnificent when they pitched their tent on the evening of the 30th December. This they did inside the same enclosure of rocks which Smyth's expedition had erected in order to protect themselves against the dry summer winds at the summit of Mt. Guajara. On this occasion the air was very cold but quite still, and the young lovers marvelled first at the clarity of the view of Teide and then at the stunning colours produced by the setting sun on the sparkling volcanic landscape. Later, huddled under a blanket with their backs on a flat rock, the couple were amazed by the brilliance of the starlit sky and by the sound of perfect silence at that height. They were also surprised by the natural warmth emanating from the volcanic basalt beneath them. What might seem to most people today a peculiar way to spend a honeymoon was, in those days of innocent exploration and discovery, most romantic.

However, it was mid-afternoon on New Year's Eve when things began to change. Burrows and his wife were riding very gently up the yellow-sand southern slopes behind Guajara. They were on their way back from exploring what is known today as the lunar landscape, an expression of surreal volcanic art just above the southern pine forests. It had been an interesting day and they were looking forward to a mug of tea brewed on a pine needle fire when they noticed strange warm gusts of wind followed by sudden chills.

The climate appeared to alter in a matter of minutes from a pleasant and sparkling winter's day into something frightening and menacing. Instinctively the horses broke into a trot before Ruth and Jamie dismounted to lead the nervous animals up the last narrow track towards their campsite. By the time they reached their tent again at the summit of Guajara an icy gale had blown up and Teide had vanished behind a dense cloud. It began to snow heavily soon afterwards and the wind screamed and whirled horribly over the sharp rock formations around them. The honeymooners huddled together in their tent. They wrapped themselves up in everything they could find and prayed the blizzard would not lift away the canvass or that the horses, sheltered behind a volcanic wall just above their enclosure, would not bolt. The storm lasted well into the night but the Englishman's little wife eventually fell asleep in his arms. She believed in his assurances that the stone enclosure built by Charles Piazzi Smyth and his party would protect them, and it did.

It was in the early hours of New Year's Day that everything suddenly went quiet on Piazzi's mountain. The wind faded as suddenly as it had blown up and Jamie was able to close his eyes. When Ruth peeped out in the morning there was bright sunlight. She discovered snowdrifts all about them, but their tent, within the primitive construction of stone walls, was intact and only appeared to have a light covering of snow. She thanked God for the astronomer's stone defences and lit a fire to brew the cup of tea they had so longed for the previous evening. She wrapped a blanket around her shoulders, took the horses some oats and brushed snow off their backs before returning to her husband. The inviting warmth within the tent and a playful lump of snow to awaken Jamie led to their honeymoon becoming much more than just romantic for the rest of the morning.

WHEN BITEN BY AN INSECT

Hugo Stratton became a regular visitor to Tenerife in the late 1920s. After developing a lung complaint during the war in the trenches he was advised that wintering in the Orotava Valley would cure him or at least improve his condition. The fact that he returned time and time again was proof, not only that he considered the climate and the air perfect for his health but that he also found Tenerife and its people a delight. In fact he became an accomplished artist during his time on the island and liked nothing more than to disappear into the hills with a mule or a horse carrying his canvass and brushes.

He was also an intrepid explorer. In November 1928, although by then he could have been driven along a winding narrow road in a motor car, Stratton borrowed a horse, as he often did, from his friend the Vice-Consul's son in Puerto de la Cruz. His sole intention was to capture the magic of the eve of Saint Andrew's at Icod de los Vinos. He had heard about *Las Tablas*. This was a different kind of fiesta, with origins in the 17th century.

Daring young men tempted fate, risked broken limbs and displayed reckless bravery hurling themselves down the steep, shiny cobbled streets at unbelievable speeds on nothing more than carefully prepared pieces of wood. The fiesta still exists today although it has perhaps become too popular and therefore less traditional.

On the way to Icod he stopped at San Juan de la Rambla to give the horse a drink from a gushing water trough which passed along a stone wall outside the old church. The temple had a quaint, picturesque interior and a curious old clock. He noticed a magnificent example of lattice-work on a balcony and thought he must draw a sketch and return to colour it on another occasion. Stratton had set out in the early morning but it was after dark when he finally reached the Milan Hotel, at the top of the main plaza in Icod. His artistic instincts and jovial conversations with country folk working in the vineyards on the way had enticed him to stop all too often. In fact the Englishman had found himself, on more than one occasion during his travels in the Canary Islands, with no option but to put up a tent in an abandoned field rather than sleep in comfort. But it was a kind of freedom he enjoyed.

The Milan Hotel cost ten pesetas a day. This included meals and a stable for the horse. It was clean and all members of the staff were eager to make him feel at home, so much so that he decided to prolong his stay for an entire week. Furthermore, Hugo thoroughly enjoyed taking part in *Las Tablas*, which he was invited to try and repeated over and over again as sips of good wine and adrenalin mingled to induce a mix of bravery and lunacy.

He also found Icod to be a place full of charm and colour and wanted to take the opportunity to paint some of the wonderful old town houses and to explore the surrounding country and coastline towards Garachico. Unfortunately, on the day he was due to saddle up to return to Puerto he woke up with a severely swollen ankle and a high temperature. A doctor was called at once and diagnosed an infection caused most probably by an insect bite. The good doctor assumed it might have been that of a flea or some other parasitic blood-sucking insect. The hotel proprietor assured *Mister* Stratton that he can't have been bitten in his hotel and that it must have been an insect that had accompanied his horse. Stratton, normally an example of courage, later recalled that he thought neither the proprietor, nor indeed the doctor, had the remotest idea about what kind of bug might have caused his sudden illness. Nevertheless they had certainly succeeded in frightened the living daylights out of him by suggesting he would just have to have whatever poison was in the ankle cut out immediately with a scalpel.

The speed with which news of the Englishman's swollen ankle spread through a town of 8,000 souls in the 1920s without the use of modern communication systems was quite astonishing. On the other hand Stratton had won himself sincere respect and recognition with his heroic runs on the night of *Las Tablas* and a man by the name of Angelo appeared at the hotel reception long before the kind doctor returned with his scalpel. The hotel proprietor permitted Angelo to look at the ankle. He knew almost immediately that the English guest had been bitten by a spider, quite a common spider in fact, as was discovered after stripping the sheets from the bed.

It was a *dendryphantes nidicolens*, a

mischievous little character often referred to as the jumping spider. Although normally quite harmless, its bite has been known to produce swelling and sore limbs in some people, especially foreign travellers with lesser resistance to allergies. It was quite evident that Stratton, having survived the savagery of the battlefield trenches of the First World War, had feeble defences against the ruthless attack of a minute spider in the middle of the night.

Angelo, with full permission from the embarrassed hotel proprietor, arranged for Hugo Stratton to be carried on the back of a cart down the hill to the tiny fishing village of San Marcos. It had grown around a small harbour built there in the 17th century for embarking wine onto English merchant ships.

Apparently a man lived there who knew all about insect bites and would cure him without having to use a knife. He had already been warned that a foreigner was on the way. The folk healer was known simply as *el picudo* because he had a long pointed nose. He was a tall, slim but strong-looking man and he stood in a green doorway waiting for them.

The first thing *el picudo* did, even before inspecting the bite, was to tell the Englishman that he should eat more vegetables and fruit because he undoubtedly had a weak liver. Taken aback, but in the slim man's hands, Hugo Stratton had no choice. He would have to accept the logic. Nevertheless he did express a polite, old-fashioned, English form of surprise when *el picudo* chewed a leaf of tobacco, spat it out onto the wooden kitchen table and rubbed the mixture of saliva and chewed tobacco onto the swollen ankle with a big brown thumb. Then, while the juice was apparently left to scare away the spider's poison, the man peeled a lemon and ground its skin together with vinegar. He put the contents into a small container and told his patient to rub some of this potion into his ankle three times a day until the swelling disappeared. In fact by sunset that evening the fever had gone and most of the swelling had vanished.

The kind doctor in Icod called in on the Milan Hotel on his way home from the surgery. Stratton invited him to a whisky and a cigar after dining. It was the politest way he could find to tell the doctor, the one who had wanted to cut the poison out with his scalpel, that his surgical skills would not be required on this occasion.

As a matter of interest the islands are still blessed with a whole variety of strange, interesting and unbelievable remedies for all kinds of insect bites. One either believes in old traditional cures or not. It depends upon the level of desperation. A mixture of thyme, oleander and vinegar is thought to keep fleas and mosquito out of the bedroom. This is not recommended for young couples hoping to enjoy a long and loving relationship. Basil is also known to do the trick. Burning twigs from the retama bush found in the volcanic landscape around Mount Teide, or leaves from a eucalyptus tree are very effective repellents.   But the most common deterrent is garlic. It is said that goatherds used to rub garlic on their flea-bitten legs before taking their goats out to graze. On the other hand, if Hugo Stratton had been to a town called Agulo on the island of La Gomera seventy years later he might have been taken to meet an interesting lady. Renowned for her cooking she was also believed to know an ancient remedy for dealing with a spider's bite. She would use ash from a fig tree mixed with a spider's own web to rub into a bite. Hugo Stratton never travelled to the other islands but returned to the Milan Hotel in Icod on many occasions, and became particularly fond of the little sandy cove at San Marcos.

LOLO THE LEGEND

It was early June 1954. The cocks crowing at each other across the Orotava Valley awakened Simon Napier long before Antonio the goatherd arrived with Pipa, Salada and Negrita. They were the three goats which usually accompanied him on his morning rounds. He milked them outside the back door once a week for María the cook and she used their milk to make her cheeses. The cows lazily swatting flies with their tails in the barn provided milk for her mistress's tea.

After filling the pewter canisters Antonio waited for Maria to give him a warm cup of *gofio* and milk and a bucket of leftovers for his pigs. This was one of the rituals of a sleepy piece of land many considered a paradise.

Simon was a young fruit importer from London and was already highly considered at Covent Garden. This was only his second visit to Tenerife and he was staying at Caledonia, a magnificent house belonging to his cousin, Rio Reid, a descendant of 19th century Scottish immigrants. Caledonia was one of a number of exceptionally beautiful mansions built in the 1930s close to the

Grand Taoro Hotel and Simon was finishing breakfast on the veranda overlooking the lush gardens. He had an appointment with an interpreter to accompany him to Los Prados, a banana plantation at Punta Brava, to the west of Puerto de la Cruz, and he was waiting for Manuel, the chauffeur, to collect him. Los Prados belonged to a very distinguished local gentleman, whose children were educated by an English governess.

Punctuality has never been a local forte but the fact that this family had an English governess led Simon Napier to believe that she might have introduced some form of discipline to the household. He was quite wrong.

When he and the interpreter arrived at the plantation punctually at ten o'clock as agreed, they were met by *el encargado*, the foreman. His employer was otherwise engaged. In other words the gentleman who owned the estate and whom he had arranged to meet had not yet risen for breakfast. Simon was informed that Don Diego would be pleased if instead he would join him for lunch at three o'clock that afternoon. The foreman, an excellent fellow by the name of Francisco, would show him the bananas. The arrangement appeared to suit the interpreter very well. Until then he had seemed decidedly nervous.

It was from Francisco that Simon learnt how it was his cousin's grandfather, Peter Reid, who had first attempted to export bananas. That was in 1878 when he was not only a respected merchant, but also Honorary British Vice-Consul. Although many local historians consider him to have been the pioneer in this trade, that particular experiment failed. Peter Reid ordered that the bananas be wrapped up in paper and straw and packed into the same wooden crates in which he had imported English porcelain. By the time they arrived at the docks in London the bananas had turned into a putrid, black purée.

Nevertheless, if it had not been the foreman showing him the process of banana growing, cutting and packing, Simon might not have encountered Lolo. After moving on from the rather sticky packing shed, in which dozens of flies seemed to circle like minute vultures, he was relieved to be led down a stone path to one of the lower fields. About a dozen men were diverting water from an irrigation channel into furrows dug in the rich soil of a banana field. Almost all of them wore magnificent handmade knives.

These hung in sheaths from strands of brown rope tied around their waists and which they also used as belts. Those ropes, he discovered later, were in fact slithers cut from the outside of banana trunks. When dried they were almost unbreakable and very useful for tying bundles together, as well as for holding up trousers around the men's slim waistlines. The clothes worn by the banana plantation workers appeared to be considerably stained. The brown marks were caused by the juices of the banana plant and were impossible to wash off.

Some of the men were using hoes to create more furrows around rows of banana plants, preparing the way for the water to soak into their roots. Others cut square slices from the banana plant trunks. They used these to dam the channels in order to divert the flow of water into separate divisions within the fields. Francisco unsheathed his own knife, wet it in the channel and sharpened it on a flat rock before showing Simon how to cut a slice off the trunk. It fitted the narrow channel almost perfectly. The Englishman was fascinated by the effectiveness of their simple methods.

Suddenly Simon heard a long mournful sound, followed by two more, short toots. It sounded like a hunting horn and came from close to the main house. Shortly afterwards there was a similar reply from somewhere in the distance.

"They are taking the water to another part of the plantation", explained the interpreter. It was also a signal for the men to stop work and to take their lunch break. The instrument used to produce the sound was a conch shell. This means of communication had been inherited from the Guanches, the original native inhabitants of the Canary Islands, who used the sound made by the shell as a warning signal. The tip of the conch's spire was broken off to provide the mouth piece through which to blow like a horn.

There was a low cloud shading the valley but it was very humid and there was a lot of sweat. They all walked back up to the packing shed and sat outside on the ground with their backs against the wall. The men unveiled small baskets, neatly packed by mothers and wives, which contained provisions for a day in the plantations. Simon politely refused their offers to share their food when his interpreter wished them *buen provecho*, bon appétit, but he ate a couple of the most delicious bananas he had ever tasted.

One of the men who had been working with the hoes was *Lolo el Niño*, Lolo the Boy. He was not much taller than any of the other men but his shoulders were twice as wide and he had heavier looking thighs than any Simon had seen on the rugby fields back home. It was a long break to compensate for the hard work and there was time for the big boy to take off his *lonas*, the cloth shoes they all wore, and to invite a few of the others to join him in a makeshift arena outside the shed.

"Lolo is a wrestler. He wants to practice before tomorrow's contest against Guimar, the strongest team from the South", explained Francisco proudly.

Lucha Canaria, Canary wrestling, is possibly the oldest organised sport in these islands and has grown in popularity since the early 1990s, when the islands' autonomous governments began to fund local traditions. One or two historians have suggested that the pyramids in Guimar betray Egyptian connections and that the origin of this particular kind of wrestling is also in Egypt.

One by one the men rolled up their trousers to well above the knees, bent over and put their cheeks against Lolo's. The wrestlers then grabbed each other's trousers with their left hand, brushed the ground with the right and commenced fighting.

The sparring partners were tripped, lifted or spun to the ground time after time as the strong one made all his weight, balance and fine skills play with his opponents. It was fun. They laughed. They cheered.

They laughed and cheered even louder, and in astonishment when, without any prompting at all, Simon Napier took off his fine English leather shoes and Jermyn Street socks and stepped into the ring to take his turn. The interpreter rolled his eyes skywards and muttered something to God and to the Englishman's mother. Lolo shrugged his shoulders and looked across at the foreman. The older man hesitated for a moment and then also shrugged his shoulders before nodding his consent.

Simon was nimble and kept his feet moving as they circled for what must have been half a minute. Wrestling is not a patient sport and a contest can be over very quickly. Indeed the Englishman suddenly found himself being spun around in the air before being landed, as gently as a feather, on the dry earth. As is the custom, Lolo helped the defeated Napier onto his feet and lifted his hand high in the air. Everyone clapped and cheered loudly and took the liberty of congratulating him. The foreigner felt quite emotional. *La lucha* was indeed a noble and beautiful sport.

"Lolo asks if you will see him fight tomorrow", said the interpreter. He would be delighted, replied *el inglés*.

Then, all of a sudden there was a stunned silence. Francisco the foreman glared at Lolo. After all, he might have been a great wrestler, but he was also a simple plantation worker.

"Lolo asks if you will take him to England", stammered the interpreter.

Naturally Simon Napier didn't quite know what to say. He was not at all sure whether to take Lolo seriously or not, but after a long look into the wrestler's eager eyes he decided to play along with him. After all, the tricky situation was entirely of his doing. He chose to put on a brave face, to take the bull by the horn and to enjoy it too.

"All right", he said, understanding from the absolute silence around him that Lolo had been very serious in his request.

"Tell him I will take him to England on two conditions. One is that he comes back to Tenerife with me on my return in six months. The other is that he must win every single one of his fights tomorrow".

Wrestlers always participate in several bouts during a contest between regions, competing against all the opponents one by one. Surely he would not win them all.

Francisco the foreman looked at Lolo. The boy nodded and the foreman formalised the agreement by shaking Simon Napier's hand. Then he begged the foreigner not to mention a word of this to his employer. The interpreter made the same request. They need not have concerned themselves. Napier was a good man and would always avoid causing anyone's trouble.

In fact he didn't even tell his cousin. This was strictly his own problem and he would have to solve it as quietly and pleasantly as he possibly could. Nevertheless, what everyone in England would say was another matter and he would meet that hurdle when he had to, if indeed he had to.

Actually Simon began to think vainly that he could help a simple banana plantation worker escape the bonds of poverty by taking him back to England with him. He could teach him English and one day employ him as his agent in the Canary Islands. However it was very rare for any wrestler to win every contest in a match. He would have to be very experienced and almost a legend.

The next day *Lolo El Niño* won every bout. Simon Napier realised he had no option. He would have to respect the agreement. He stood up, took a deep breath and walked across the dusty arena with the interpreter to congratulate Lolo, prepared to face the consequences. But the wrestler just smiled and then looked over to the crowd which stood on a dry patch of grassland. A lovely young face with heavy dark eyebrows and big brown eyes smiled back and then lowered her head modestly.

"I am sorry *señor*. I cannot go with you. I cannot leave my *novia* here. My best friend likes her too and if I go with you he will take her from me. I am sorry, *señor*."

Lolo did become a legend. He and that girl with the brown eyes were married before too long. Simon was an honoured guest at the wedding and within a year the couple had gone to England and Scotland as his guests. They developed a great admiration for each other in spite of cultural, economic and language barriers. Today, Lolo's oldest daughter teaches English at a local school in the north of Tenerife and one of his sons, Luis, owns a thriving *tapas* restaurant in London's Stockwell Road. Simon Napier, who never had children of his own, is an old man now but Luis and his own family often go to stay at the Napier's farm in the Scottish Borders. For fifteen years Simon bought bananas for the London markets from the gentleman who owned the Los Prados banana plantations. He was never tempted to tell the banana grower how delighted he had been with his lack of English punctuality, and that it had been the foreman who had shown him round the estate that day early in June 1954.

OLD WIVES TALE ON SORE HEADS

When James Young decided to visit his relatives in Puerto de la Cruz in 1932, travelling was still relatively adventurous and infinitely more relaxing. Although the political situation in Europe was once again beginning to stir up grave predictions, and Spain was brewing for its bloody civil war, the Canary Islanders still remained relatively untouched by major power struggles. Ordinary folk, unhampered by the vast wealth obtained by privileged landowners, maintained the very passive, gentle and hospitable way of life for which they were known.

James arrived on a Yeoward Line steamer from Liverpool, with a one way passage bought at the company's office at Nº 24, James Street. It was a hot and sticky late October day in Santa Cruz but by the time the *guagua*, a rickety bus, had struggled up the hill and dropped him in La Laguna for the sum of just one peseta the climate had totally changed. It felt quite cold and it was almost as damp and foggy as the Mersey he had left behind. It was also drizzling hard when James stepped into the Aguerre Hotel in the early evening, and a bitter wind was blowing down from the mountain range to the north of the town. The *guaguas* did not travel at night and he had been well advised to make an overnight stop at La Laguna. The road to the Orotava Valley, he was told by a fellow passenger, wound tediously in and out of the ravines and could be quite hazardous in the wet.

The Aguerre Hotel today remains very much as it was in 1932. It has managed to maintain a charming and traditional old time, Spanish feel about it. It was built in 1760 as the town residence of Don Cesáreo de la Torre y Ceballos, Captain of the Guimar Regiment and Member of the Royal Economic Society of La Laguna. Before being converted into a hotel in 1885, the Aguerre Continental, as it was known originally, had also been the official residence of the Bishop of Tenerife. Judging from entries into the hotel's first visitor's book, some guests felt quite in awe at the thought of spending a night as a guest of His Excellency.

But James Young was still only twenty five and rather neglectful of religion. So he was not going to seek innocent seclusion and religious contemplation inside the Aguerre. Instead he hungered for amusement and for a first taste of real local character. He enquired where he might enjoy a hot meal and a jug of the best wine in the town, having recently read Barlow's Journal. This was a diary kept by a sailor who frequently travelled to the Canaries in the 17th century and mentioned the island's wines with fondness. James was also reasonably cultured and therefore imagined he might discover the sweet taste of Malmsey, the wine Tenerife was so famous for three or four centuries ago and which William Shakespeare paid tribute to in his Merry Wives of Windsor and Twelfth Night.

Although the hotel proprietor appeared slightly offended by his guest's preference not to dine at the hotel, he reluctantly told Mr. Young that Marcelino's house, in a narrow alley just down the cobbled street towards the cathedral, was the place he was looking for.

It had stopped drizzling but there was still a bitter chill in the wind and it threatened heavier rain. In fact there were downpours for eleven consecutive days and nights in La Laguna during October 1932 and old newspaper articles remember a kind of dampness which penetrated right to people's bones.

James buttoned up his coat and walked briskly towards the cathedral before turning left into the narrow alley. Marcelino's tavern was dimly lit by a couple of paraffin lamps. The doorway betrayed a rough environment but the aroma from the kitchen and the din of voices gave him an even greater appetite.

He ordered a cup of wine and was brought a whole jug. It accompanied a stew of lentils, pork and potatoes. He had never eaten *lentejas* and there did not seem to be any choice. Nevertheless, by the look of his plate, wiped clean with bread, he had never tasted anything so delicious.

Sadly the wine in 1932 was nothing like Malmsey. It was almost vinegar, doped with sulphur and certainly dangerous. But a young man like James, with a rebel in his heart, would never leave his glass empty. After one glassful the venomous wine quickly dampened his senses and turned miraculously into the juice of paradise. He downed the whole jug and even more after being invited to drink with Marcelino and his friends.

When someone knocked on the door of his hotel room on the following morning, he felt as if something was hammering from very deep inside his head.

"*La guagua.* It waits for you, *señor!*"

"Tell it to leave without me," he felt like saying. But it was the hotel proprietor's voice and he did not want to be the kind provider of cheap satisfaction. Besides, James might have been reckless at times but he was still a gentleman and the bus driver and the curious passengers had had the decency to wait for him. They were also kind enough, at least to begin with, not to try to ask the foreigner too many questions, especially after they learnt he was suffering from such a terrible *resaca* obtained at Marcelino's.

Most of the locals were on their way to the towns of Tacoronte and La Orotava and the chance for some light hearted mockery eventually got the better of them. One or two were cruel enough to suggest that the wine in Tacoronte was much the best, and that he should never have touched the poison Marcelino had offered him. James soon began to wonder if the hotel proprietor had not sent him there with ill intent, in revenge for his not dining at the Aguerre.

The North road, in 1932, was just as one would imagine. Apart from meandering eternally, it was rocky and muddy. James had not been seasick crossing the Bay of Biscay but his stomach turned in and out of the corners and up and down in the dips, and both it and his head skidded across the muddy stretches. He felt very sorry for himself and there could be no possible remedy for his sore head after having it rattled and bumped into another, yet unexplored condition.

Antonio, the driver, felt pity on the poor, innocent foreigner. Consequently, when they made a scheduled halt at the central square at Tacoronte he beckoned the foolish *inglés* to follow him away from the bus.

"*Venga*", he beckoned, and introduced him to a plump, colourful lady with two enormous baskets at her feet. Descendants of this wonderful woman called Catalina can still be seen and heard at street corners in Tacoronte claiming in a style reminiscent of the best sopranos that they have fresh sardines or mackerel for sale.

After Antonio's explanations and some considerable waving of arms James was taken through a doorway and into a room. With a petrifying screech the woman ordered him to lie down on a wooden bench.

Any reasonable man would have declined politely or fled in terror, especially as the room became crowded with other women, all plump, all exhibiting magnificent wrestlers arms, all yelling at each other and all giving off the unmistakeable odour of a fish market. But in his condition James was beyond reasoning. Besides, what would his relatives in Puerto de la Cruz think when he arrived that afternoon in time for tea, if he was delivered alive at all, with such evident signs of having consumed enormous quantities of wine on his very first night on the island? It would not be a happy start. They were very Presbyterian.

Sore heads resulting from the taking of excess alcohol or from the drinking of poor wine are common amongst visitors to the Canary Islands in these days of modern tourism. But, as James found out, local islanders knew all about them too.

The shrieking and highly amused women were thankfully ushered out of the room and James suddenly felt a curious numb tranquillity as the high pitched conference ceased and his ears became accustomed to an ominous silence. But relief was only momentary because an old wives tale was about to be put to the test.

In earlier days it was believed that if one were to place a half-filled glass of cool water upside down upon a damp cloth on the top of a poor individual's head, whilst prayers were murmured in accompaniment, the heat and turmoil in the head would cause the water inside the glass to bubble and thus evaporate the evil. There does not appear to be any written proof to suggest that this method was based on sound scientific principles and this particular fishwife had inherited what was certainly a much more natural technique for curing the common hangover.

"*Tranquilito*. Take it easy!" said Catalina in a surprisingly soothing voice considering her customary shouting.

As she spoke she waved about a huge knife with one hand. In the other she held a well-proportioned potato.

I have still not found words to express what might have gone through young James's head in that instant. But, as I have already said, he was by no means a timid man and in fact he really began to accept that the big woman with the fearful knife and the potato had the kindest of intentions. She somehow balanced her wide buttocks upon a minute milking stool and deliberately set about cutting the large potato into slices. Then she placed them neatly across his forehead and upon his temples. When she was satisfied she took off her old headscarf, shook a number of fish scales out of it, and wrapped it around his head to hold the slices of potato in place.

In spite of the uncomfortable wooden bench, James dozed off soon after the fishwife had left him on his own. When he awakened, a ray of afternoon sunlight was peeping through a small window and Catalina was sitting on the stool over a pail of water. She was using the same huge knife with surgical expertise to cut open and gut a variety of freshly caught fish. She looked up at him and offered a smile as warm as the ray of sunlight. The *guagua* had been gone a long time and so had his sore head.

MARIA THE FISHERWOMAN

In the Canary Islands, before the refrigerator became common to most households, it was the custom to keep freshly bought fish in a special cupboard protected by mosquito netting or on a table in a cool place. The cupboard or table legs were placed in containers of water to prevent harvesting ants from getting to the source of interest.

The fish wouldn't stay fresh for very long in these conditions, but it didn't seem to matter. They were often salted to preserve them for long periods. This was done by first covering them with a thick layer of sea salt. Then they were sun-dried before the excess salt was washed off with a mixture of water and vinegar.

In Port Orotava there was also a thriving little fleet of fishing boats and it was customary for local women to gather around the harbour on the day they wanted fish for the family meal. They knew that on most days their fishermen returned with a good catch and a wide choice. When enough had been caught a boat would return to port where the fisherman and his assistant would roll up their trouser legs, jump into the sea and manhandle their boat onto the pebbles. They would then rely on friends, relatives or passers-by with nothing better to do to help haul it out of reach of the high tide.

The fishmongers today have their stalls in the municipal marketplace, a mile or two from the port, which is now known as Puerto de la Cruz. Most of the fish they sell is frozen, imported or purchased from the fish farms which have sprung up along the south coast of Tenerife in recent years. But they do still have a limited amount of locally caught favourites on show, like the *vieja*, a parrotfish. In the 1960s there was a market beside the town hall, and the fishmongers shared space with haggling North African traders.

But the fish market originally stood where one might expect to find it, right on the harbour. It was just above where the fishing boats were pulled up onto the pebbles, across the harbour from the Royal Customs House and almost where an inn called *La Fragata* stands today.

The fishmongers were invariably the wives, sisters or mothers of fishermen. They were a cheerful lot and they made a good living from the hard work of their men.

Five or six of these stalwart women usually defended the stalls and there was always a throng of a lesser breed of women examining and selecting their fish. Some of the regular clients used the occasion to catch up on gossip. They could spend an entire morning spreading the news with a glorious use of arms and potent voices, whilst children hung on to aprons or played at the water's edge. These were the ordinary housewives.

They bought anything from a delicious *sama*, a pink dentex, to the everlasting mackerel. Then there were the servants sent by wealthy mistresses who could never be seen mingling with such a crowd. Naturally they would order the best of the catch and the fishmongers made certain they paid handsomely for the privilege. That might be the *cabrillo*, the black-tail comber. It is very similar to, if not better in taste, than the whiting or grey mullet. Affluent households would never touch the chicharro, the blue jack mackerel. It was considered rather common. However, there was a time when members of the privileged classes in the Canaries wouldn't touch fish at all. Fish attracted flies and was only fit for the lower classes.

After the volcanic eruption in 1706 which destroyed the old harbour at Garachico on the north east of Tenerife, Orotava became the island's main trading port after Santa Cruz. It also provided a popular landing place for the many intrepid travellers and explorers from Victorian Britain. They came on merchant ships or on handsome private yachts and were ferried ashore from their anchorage by fleets of rowing boats whenever the sea permitted.

In the summer of 1878, a magnificent schooner anchored just out from the harbour. From the moment she was spotted, approaching in full sail along the northern coastline, she became a source of admiration and attracted visitors from all over the island.

She was The Sunbeam and belonged to Lord Brassey, Baron of Bulkely in Cheshire. Her white hull gleamed in the morning sunlight.

The sea was a flat calm and his elegant and attractive wife, Lady Annie, asked to be rowed ashore as soon as the formalities had been completed at the Royal Customs House. She took her children on what she referred to as an educational expedition. At the top of the harbour steps their attention was immediately drawn to the commotion around those women in their blood-stained aprons. In spite of her graceful poise and beauty, Lady Brassey was a resolute character and very capable of exploring different customs. She mingled enthusiastically with the local women and they welcomed her with admiring looks. She decided to order five or six good sized hake for the captain and senior crew members from one of the knife-wielding women.

That was María. She was the oldest, plumpest,

jolliest and fiercest looking of the five fishmongers, and she promptly chopped off their heads with what could only be described as a machete. It fell with the speed of a guillotine. She then sliced them open and let their guts fall, with a bloody splash, into a tin container on the ground. The tin was then picked up by a skinny eight year old girl. She was the plump woman's granddaughter and she was also called María.

Moments later, as they left the harbour, Lady Brassey and her children were passed by two thin, barefooted boys. They were carrying a simple wire net suspended from the middle of a long, wooden stick. Each boy carried one end of the stick on their shoulders. María, the skinny fishmonger's granddaughter, walked alongside them with the tin containing the insides of the fish which Lady Brassey had ordered.

The visitor was taken aback but rather impressed by the very English looking hat with a blue bow which the girl was wearing. She assumed it must have been handed down to a servant by one of the British residents who lived in one of the grand mansions in the Orotava Valley. Nevertheless, she felt great sympathy in her rather superior manner.

"Those poor children", remarked Lady Annie. "They look so terribly thin and undernourished."

A couple of mornings later the distinguished English visitor and her children saw the same three urchins transporting the same net and the tin container past the fishmongers and away from the harbour. She decided to follow them as far as the small cliff below the little chapel of San Telmo, just to the east of the port. They watched from above as the three children set up what was evidently a most ingenious device with which to catch fish.

They attached the wire net to one end of the long stick and dropped it into a deep pond in the rock pools. The boys placed the middle part of the stick into a groove in a rock and stood beside the other end, which they could barely reach by standing on their toes. The net was then lowered delicately into the pond. María, the skinny girl, then threw something bloody which she plucked out of the tin container into the middle of the sunken net. She was evidently the leader of this particular gang of young fishers. She held her hand up and almost immediately yelled out an order and lowered her hand again fast. In response, the two boys tugged the end of the stick downwards using all their strength and weight to pull it down. This action quickly levered up the net, heavy with tiny jumping fish, from within the rock pool.

It was known as using the *palanca* or lever method. Lady Brassey and her children watched in absolute amazement. The three fishers gathered around the landed net and proceeded to pick out certain sizes and colours of fish which they then mercifully threw back into the rock pool. They repeated the procedure over and over again. When they were completely satisfied they headed back to Maria's stall where they emptied their catch into a wooden tray. Apparently these tiddlers, fried up in garlic, were a treat in poorer households. They were never sold, but given away to the less fortunate. Lady Annie was never told of this good act of charity and continued to grow concerned about how thin María, her two cousins and so many other local children appeared to be, ignoring the fact that her own children were just as skinny and healthy under all the immaculate clothes they wore.

After witnessing the miracle of the rock pool again three or four days later, the charming English lady got her steward to send for some local bread rolls, which she found somewhat sour in taste. The steward was to have them filled with tender slices of beef which he personally purchased at the butcher's, a sparklingly clean shop next to a Mr. Audley Sparrow's store where drawn thread work linen goods were manufactured and sold. Lady Brassey, who purchased some very pretty table cloths from Mr. Sparrow, intended to give one of these impressive and nourishing *bocadillos* to María and the two boys every day until the Sunbeam departed for the southern hemisphere. She couldn't bear to see such thin looking children every time she came ashore.

The next morning Lady Brassey waited beside the fish stalls until María arrived to collect the tin of leftovers for her net. To everyone's astonishment and under the falcon-like eye of the grandmother, she presented the young fisher with a bundle containing the rolls. They had been lovingly stuffed with the finest beef to be found on the island. The occasion took on an almost regal ceremony, and the customary din around the stalls turned into something reminiscent of a whispering courtroom.

At mid-day Lady Brassey and her children were returning from a magnificent mansion on the La Paz estate at the top of the cliff overlooking the bay. They had been invited there by a Spanish marchioness to take morning coffee. They stopped at the San Telmo chapel and looked down at the rock pools again. Her three skinny urchins were there as usual. On this occasion they all appeared to be in a high state of excitement. María was so distracted that she had forgotten all about her role as team leader. She was jumping up and down at the edge of their deep pond and the two boys were peering round the rock in astonishment, their levering stick left completely unattended. Lady Brassey and her children glanced at each other. There was no doubt in their minds that they should take a closer look. They clutched their way down the narrow path to the rock pools, and then hopped awkwardly from rock to rock with their beautiful English shoes and raised skirts towards that favourite pond.

They were dumfounded and equally excited by what they saw. Instead of dozens of tiny fry of all shapes and colours, the surface above the net was a mass of large silvery fish, eagerly feasting on the bait which had been thrown in by María. If there were any of the variety intended for the less fortunate households, they were hidden by the turmoil of flashing silver feeding on something at the surface. María's excitement was not only a consequence of the size and quantity of the fish they were about to haul out of the pond, but also because they were fully grown *lisa*, grey mullet. These were normally very difficult to capture and highly sought after by the wealthy households. It was going to be a very profitable catch.

"Mama?" questioned one of Lady Brassey's children, pointing at the bait being sucked at by the frenzy of silvery fish within the perimeter of the net. "Isn't that one of the meat rolls you gave that girl this morning?"

Indeed it was, and if one is fortunate enough today, one can often see an old woman at a rock pool that has survived the building of a modern tourist resort in Puerto. That will be another María. She will have a smaller net attached to a bamboo cane and she will be using a loaf of white bread to catch *lisa* for her own frying pan. It has become a family tradition passed down since the days when the Sunbeam anchored off Port Orotava during her eleven month ocean voyage.

THE LADY AND THE GOAT

Pamela Sommerville was making scones when she heard a familiar bleating and tinkling coming up the lane. This was followed by a shouted *"buenos días señora!"* at the gate.

It was Erasmo, the old farm caretaker. As usual, he was followed by Nina, the goat. Nina was his favourite goat. Erasmo had been retired for a year or two and his son now looked after the Sommerville's farm in the hills. When he decided to sell the herd to his cousin he had not had the heart to part with Nina. She was more like a faithful dog although a touch more mischievous.

Nina carried on bleating happily on the cement patio outside the simple country cottage and her bell tinkled with every shake of her greying head after Erasmo entered the señora's kitchen and sat down at the old wooden table without being invited to.

Mrs. Sommerville was that kind of boss. Their relationship spanned a good twenty years, and began when her husband Jim bought the farm and took him on as caretaker. Erasmus's father had worked for the previous owner of the estate and he had grown up in its fields and orchards. His inherited knowledge of agriculture, especially fruit production in this part of the island, had been a godsend. Erasmus also knew exactly how to handle the men and women who worked in the orchards. He was kind and generous but tough when necessary. A certain skill was required at times and orders from a local Canary Islander were always better accepted than when they came from a foreigner. Besides, he was well liked and admired for his understanding of the weather conditions and when to do what with the crops.

The Sommervilles retired to Tenerife in the early 1960s and owned a house just outside Puerto de la Cruz. But they loved to spend the weekends at Las Aguas. It was a small farm just below the pines, and the fruit they grew and honey they produced sold well at the markets.

Eighteen months after Jim Sommerville died Pamela began to stay for more prolonged periods at the farm and often received visits from her friends. A few of her Spanish lady friends were coming to tea that very afternoon. That is why she was busy making those scones.

"*Escones!*" said Erasmo with a wide grin after spotting the flour, the butter and the oven tray on the kitchen table.

"I've got a *merienda* this afternoon, Erasmo. Please tell Andrés to leave the gate open".

Knowing how much the old fellow liked her scones, Pamela always made a few extra and he would not leave her kitchen until she had baked them. She took off her precious engagement ring, a simple, delicate piece of jewellery with a small but valuable diamond, and put it on the window ledge before washing her hands to mix the dough. It was the usual routine before one of her tea parties. She had worn the diamond alongside her wedding ring since the day her darling Jim died. It was her way of having him close and it comforted her.

After a while she took the first tray of scones out of the oven and put them on the window ledge too. She hummed to herself as she prepared more flour and butter for the next tray of her delicious and famous scones. They had become very popular amongst her Spanish friends. In the meantime Erasmo talked away without catching his breath, as he always did, about the good old days and complaining, as he always did, about the new days.

But suddenly the English lady, who was very nimble for her age, leapt across the kitchen towards the window shouting "Erasmo, *la cabra*! Nina! Your damned goat!"

"*Qué*? *Qué pasa*?" Erasmo shouted back in alarm as if Mount Teide had erupted. The poor man was so startled by his lady's speed of movement and shouting that he fell off the chair with a solid bump before pulling himself up awkwardly and disappearing out of the kitchen to blaspheme furiously at Nina the goat.

The old goat had spotted and smelt the freshly baked scones on the window ledge and very quickly devised that if she stood on her hind legs she could reach out with her long tongue and help herself. She liked the English lady's scones too. Nina got away with it and so did Erasmo. In fact he and Pamela Sommerville enjoyed a long and hearty laugh before he wandered off down the hill with his *escones* and a potato-sack full of rubbish to get rid of. His bleating, tinkling and flatulent goat followed close behind.

But the tea party that afternoon was not as happy as usual. Although the Spanish guests found their English friend as pleasant and interesting as ever, and her scones topped with delicious homemade blackberry jam, Pamela appeared to be tired and slightly distracted. She didn't seem to have her usual delightful wit about her that afternoon and her voice sounded slightly emotional at times. Understandably, being members of the gentle sex, the ladies could not possibly depart that evening without asking Pamela whether anything was troubling her.

"It's Jims's engagement ring. I don't know what I've done with it. I know I took it off to make the scones this morning but I've been going absolutely mad looking for it all day. I have a dreadful feeling Erasmo must have taken it with the rubbish and I daren't ask him in case he thinks I am accusing him of stealing it."

The Spanish ladies glanced at each other with prolonged and knowing looks. There was no need to ask their opinion. They mistrusted mountain folk like Erasmo.

They were respectable town ladies and usually surrounded by servants in uniform. If it wasn't for their good friend, Pamela, they would never dream of being driven by their chauffeurs up into the hills along dusty tracks far away from their comfortable town houses.

Nevertheless they all got on their hands and knees to search for the missing ring. This was something they would never be seen dead doing in front of their servants or anyone else for that matter. They looked in every corner and under every piece of furniture. But it could not be found and Pamela Sommerville feared the worst. She decided not to ask Erasmo. He would never have taken it anyway. It would break his heart if he felt she had even a hint of suspicion that he might have taken it, even by accident. He was a good man who adored his English employer.

However, a couple of sleepless nights later it suddenly occurred to Pamela Sommerville that the ring might have fallen into the sink from the kitchen window ledge and it may well have got stuck in the drains. There was a ray of hope and she sent a message to Erasmo for someone to come and open up the drains immediately.

Not an hour had passed when she heard the goat bleating and tinkling up the lane and Erasmo came to the back door.

Pamela peered over his shoulder, presuming he had brought the plumber with him. But he hadn't. Instead he just stood there grinning at her from the doorway without uttering a word. In fact his face was a picture of bliss. The old man was beaming like one of his famous apples and the English lady assumed he was just very pleased with himself because he had brought her a basket full of the season's first crop of huge, golden plums. But he placed these on the kitchen table and carried on looking at his señora with what she began to consider to be a ridiculous grin.

For a horrible moment Pamela Sommerville thought the man had been drinking. After all his cheeks were rather red and it was one of those unceasing grins which characterise someone propping up the bar after a wedding. She glared at him to show that she was in no mood for any nonsense. But Erasmo beckoned her to follow him out onto the patio and she did so with a very irritable, Spanish kind of shrug of her shoulders.

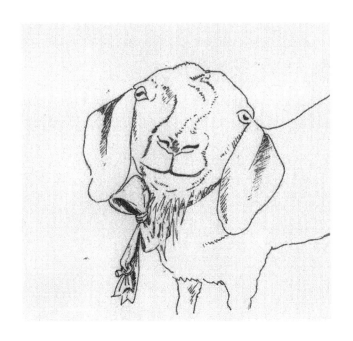

Still grinning and without uttering a single word, the old man then pointed at Nina the goat and invited Pamela to have a close look at the lovely new, red ribbon hanging around the animal's neck. She knew she didn't have choice and, as polite and kind as ever, not allowing any hint of her growing irritation to blemish her English courtesy, she bent down. Then she suddenly let out a cry and sat down clumsily on the ground hugging the goat. Pamela Sommerville shook with emotion and tears began streaming down her face. Old Erasmo also started sobbing like a little boy in between more grinning and spasms of incomprehensible words.

"Oh, Jim!" cried Pamela. Her precious engagement ring dangled, sparkling in the morning sunlight from the red ribbon. A scone was not the only thing Nina the goat had found interesting on the window ledge. She had also swallowed the ring. A few minutes later Pamela and Erasmo sat down at the kitchen table and he proceeded to go into every detail about how he had spotted something glistening in the sunlight in one of Nina's droppings down by the chicken run that very morning.

FIESTA

It was the early 1970s when a middle-aged English couple wandered across from the new San Antonio Hotel to savour a touch of old colonialism at the British Games Club in Puerto de la Cruz. They ordered gin and tonics, to which they were not especially accustomed, and walked up the steps to the tennis courts from where they heard very enthusiastic applause. Acknowledging whispered greetings, the visitors sat down on immaculately painted, green benches to watch an entertaining game of mixed doubles alongside a number of club members.

After a few minutes they began to hear what sounded like heavy gunfire in the distance. It was their first time in Tenerife and the couple looked at each other in a rather startled manner whilst the other spectators continued to enjoy the tennis and to applaud as if the thunder of exploding shells were quite normal. At the end of a game and whilst the players were changing ends, the visiting gentleman couldn't bear it anymore and decided to enquire.

"Excuse me, what are all those explosions about?" he asked the man wearing whites and a matching Panama hat who was sitting beside him on the bench.

"Oh, nothing to worry about old chap…. just the natives attacking again!" replied the club member casually in his best colonial accent before promptly standing up and wandering off down the steps to the bar, leaving the visitor and his wife open mouthed and confused.

The colonial, who apparently always liked to watch some tennis after his game of bowls, returned a few minutes later. He wore a broad smile and the twinkle in his eye betrayed a mischievous sense of humour. He was followed by Manuel, the barman, carrying a tray with two more gin and tonics for the innocent English couple. He thought it had been long enough for them to digest the thought of the attacking natives and whether or not they should speak to their Thompson's representative about shortening the holiday. He explained that it was not gunfire at all but fireworks high on the ridge at La Guancha. The low cloud hanging in the valley did indeed make them thud like distant exploding shells. He had been in the war, don't you know.

"Fireworks…in the middle of the day?" asked the tourist in disbelief.

"It's a fiesta, old chap. They set off fireworks at all hours here, especially during a fiesta. They do it to make noise. They love noise. I'm afraid they can't live without making noise. My wife loves a good fiesta. Personally, I hate them."

Sitting on the next bench and unable to ignore the conversation was the wife of another old resident and she began to chuckle. She remembered her first experience of a local fiesta twenty years earlier when they arrived in Tenerife after one of the coldest Dartmoor winters on record. One of the first things they decided to do was to go to the San Isidro fiesta in La Orotava on a very hot June day. They packed themselves, their daughter, the obedient black Labrador and provisions into the car before driving up into the old town centre.

Just outside the upper part of the town anxious shepherds, goatherds and cowmen had begun to gather their oxen, goats, mules and donkeys on a country lane. The animals wore beautifully coloured rugs on their backs and whole families stood about dressed gaily in traditional Canary garments, mingling with all the livestock. Panniers full of fruit were being strapped to the donkeys whilst bullocks, thrashing their tails against stinging flies, were being harnessed to magnificently adorned carts. They were being made ready for the *romería*, a colourful procession through the streets representing agricultural and other scenes from island life.

The family from Devon, who had made certain of learning an adequate amount of Spanish before settling on the island and Jan, their patient and understanding dog, found a good position from which to view the procession. In fact a very kind and proud lady let them share the raised position of her front door steps. They had already been invited by welcoming townsfolk to share wine, chick peas, cheese and balls of *gofio* when the proceedings began.

The swaying procession flowed down the cobbled streets like an undulating sea of colour and sound. Most of the men wore black fedora hats, white shirts, woollen breeches and scarlet cummerbunds. The girls also bloomed in rich scarlet waistcoats over their gypsy blouses, and their striped woven dresses covered exquisite petticoats.

There was much singing and even more laughter. Ripples of admiration greeted the beautifully adorned carts and strong men led their massive bullocks, leaning against their necks whenever they needed to stop or to slow them down. Lovely girls offered even more wine, fruit and delicious morsels of grilled meat prepared at the rear of carts which made their jerky way down the cobbles.

The English family were feeling so much at ease, loving every second and totally absorbed by the charms of a real Spanish fiesta. It was such tremendous fun.

But suddenly it happened. The first giant firework shot skywards and offered a deafening explosion immediately above their heads. They should have known better. Although he was well accustomed to the sound of shotguns during pheasant shoots on the moors, Jan objected, bolted across the merry procession and disappeared.

"Jan, Jan, Jan" called the English lady cutting through the same colourful procession after the dog. She was followed in the same direction, but much more discretely, by her husband and daughter.

"I'll bet he's waiting for us at the car", she shouted back, trying to be reassuring while shoving her way through the masses in what, to any onlooker, appeared to be a state of panic. People shrugged their shoulders and remarked, *"Son ingléses"* to explain the strange behaviour.

The foreign lady was almost right. Like any well trained hunting dog, the black Labrador had gone straight to where they had parked the car. Unfortunately it was someone else's car it had got into. It was a big, black saloon and all its doors were locked. How on earth did Jan get into it? Somebody said the car belonged to a man called Paco and that he was bound to be at the bar on the square. The Englishman and his daughter strode off in that direction, leaving the wife to talk nicely at her dog through a rear window.

A short time later two smiling local gentlemen ambled up. They stared at the car for a moment with slightly bloodshot eyes and then gazed endlessly at the lady who was talking to the dog that was inside the car. She could feel how desperately they were trying to concentrate. After all it was an unusual situation for two drunks to deal with, but she was foolish enough to try to explain her predicament without being asked to.

"Never mind, señora, we will help you. You wait here. We will come back", one of them offered just before another huge firework exploded.

The English lady was just congratulating herself for their departure when they returned, one of them carrying a ghastly little brown dog with protruding teeth in his arms.

"Here you are, we have found your dog", he said, holding it out towards her.

"I have not lost my dog. That is my dog in the car. I have lost the owner of the car and the car is locked with my dog inside it. *Adios*. Please, *adios*!" she begged, and looked around at the gathering crowd of amused spectators. A firework went off.

"Why don't you want this dog? We found it for you!" one of the two *amigos* said accusingly. They stood there swaying for a minute or two thinking, and then one of them repeated, "You wait here. We will return. We know where to find you another dog!" They looked around them at the spectators with widening grins on their faces.

"I don't want a dog. My husband is finding the man who owns this car. *Adios*", the English señora insisted very loudly. Bang went another firework and the two men wandered off to the bar again.

At that point a Guardia Civil policeman approached and enquired "*Que pasa?*" She told him.

"Ah-h-h-h-h!" he exclaimed. "That is Don Angel's car. He has just been to the plaza with his wife, but how did your dog get into his car if it was locked?" he asked with a definite hint of suspicion in his eye.

The English lady thought their troubles were over at last simply because a policeman had taken an interest, but she waited and waited. Half an hour later her husband and daughter returned. They both looked tired and very irritable, particularly the husband. They had been to the house of Paco but he was out. In any case Paco's car was green. This one was black. She explained that the policeman had said it belonged to Don Angel, so her husband grunted and went off to look for Don Angel. Unfortunately Don Angel was also out and his servants said he might be *anywhere*. He was that kind of angel.

A man in the crowd offered to smash the car window. Another said he would get a wire. Someone said he knew a man who was good with hinges. Another firework shook the proceedings just when the two *amigos* ambled up to the car again.

"Does it wear a collar, *señora*?" the braver of the two asked kindly.

"I have not lost my dog!" she retaliated, not knowing whether to laugh or cry. "I have found my dog. I am waiting for my husband!" A very loud firework ended her sentence.

"I told you," said the other drunk, "*La pobre mujer* has lost her husband, not her dog. You wait señora!" They wandered off, determinedly this time, and were back before long. On this occasion they were accompanied by an extremely tall, blond man with a very red face.

"Señora. He is here. We have found your husband for you!"

"Bonjour, madame", said the foreign stranger very courteously indeed. "These two men told me you are looking for me". In fact the poor man, a Swiss resident, had merely been having a beer or two at a corner bar when the two local gentlemen stepped in. They had assumed by his foreign appearance that he must without a doubt have been the missing husband, and dragged him along.

Another loud firework exploded as the English husband came around the corner. He took surprisingly little interest in the two drunks and in the foreigner his wife was talking to in a very animated manner and suggested he take his family home and return later to look for Don Angel. However, at that moment another man parked his car alongside the black saloon. Hearing about the predicament he invited the lady to sit in it, where the dog could see her, while her husband resumed the search for Don Angel. This gesture, which was accepted gratefully, and the sincere assistance offered by the two drunks, was typical of the kindness of Canary Islanders. Meanwhile, as the English husband continued looking for Don Angel and everyone waited for the tale to end happily, all sorts of rumours were being whispered about what the almost certainly innocent Don Angel was doing, where and with whom. The drunks became drunker and brought more dogs and one or two husbands for the English lady to inspect. The policeman came by again and shrugged his shoulders, and a number of fireworks made people jump every now and then.

Jan the Labrador had given up hope and curled himself up on the rear seat of Don Angel's car.

It was late evening when the English husband returned. His wife was about to accept the sensible alternative, which was to be driven home whilst he waited by the car. But a tall, thin looking man with a delightful face strolled up and surprised them in perfect English. "You are looking for me. My name is Angel López. I understand you think I have a dog for sale!" Before the English couple could reply, a volley of fireworks thundered in the sky marking a triumphant end to the fiesta.

THE MAIL BOAT

The fast ferry was gathering speed as it turned towards Grand Canary at the mouth of the harbour. A magnificent, overpopulated modern cruise liner lay extravagantly against the south dock and a pilot boat rushed, tossing in the ferry's wake, towards a giant, black ship, top-heavy with containers.

It was early autumn at the harbour in Santa Cruz and the speed of activity in 2005 contrasted with the relic of history sitting in dry dock. Alonso Valcárcel, an elegant old gentleman in his seventies and a much younger foreigner gazed at the La Palma from beside a row of dirty and rusty Korean fishing vessels which were making ready for their next trawl along the African coast. In fact both men considered themselves foreigners although each had close ties with Tenerife. Alonso had spent the last fifty years making a fortune in Venezuela and had returned to the Canaries in 2003 to escape what he considered to be the madness of the Hugo Chavez regime. The younger man was an ex- Royal Navy Captain. His name was James Reid and his descendents had lived in Puerto de la Cruz since the middle of the nineteenth century.

As the two men walked under the La Palma's

burgundy hull a tear betrayed the old gentleman and James broke the ice.

"She certainly does have the most beautiful lines and I can see why you think she should be restored to her former glory!"

The La Palma used to be known simply as the mail boat. In her proud days of duty she spent her life hopping between the Canary Islands carrying people, cargo and the mail. She was a lifeline between the islands in the days when people rarely travelled and when aeroplanes were just beginning to be thought of as a convenient mode of transport. The mail boat began her life in 1912 and made her last crossing in 1972. She was built by W. Harkness and Son Ltd, of Middlesborough, and was ordered by Elder Dempster's partners in Tenerife in order to improve trade between the islands. It was sad to see the good old boat dying slowly in a corner of the port. That is why the regional government and local businessmen set up the Foundation for the La Palma

Mail Boat in 2003. Their aim was to turn her into a working museum of island shipping.

"I asked you to come along today James, not because you are an experienced seaman and I think you should join the Foundation, but because I'd like you to know why I will always be indebted to your family."

Alonso invited his younger friend to a simple fish lunch at San Andrés, just along the coast from the port. The story unfurled in the sea breeze under a canopy of palm leaves, whilst cool wine accompanied fried sardines and octopus soaked in olive oil and vinegar.

James's family once imported goods from around the world, and exported fruit to the British Isles and onion seed across the Atlantic to clients in Texas. His Uncle Tom often went across to the island of La Palma to haggle with banana growers for a good price and in search of the finest fruit. He represented buyers in London and Glasgow.

It was a stormy December night, just before Christmas in 1950, when he was aboard the La Palma mail boat returning to Tenerife. He had dined well and was ready to retire to his bunk. However, there were too many people being sea sick, including the man sharing his cabin, so he thought it would be best to get some fresh air.

The crew knew Tom Reid well. They were accustomed to him going on deck in all weathers to get his sea legs or even to remain there for the duration of the overnight passage. But there was a big swell that night, the rain was lashing down and there was thunder and lightning. Only an Englishman could be foolish enough to want to walk out on deck for some fresh air on a night like this, but no doubt the La Palma's Captain would ask him onto the bridge if he was in a good mood and felt like sharing a whisky. He often did.

Tom was well wrapped up in his London raincoat and he was enjoying the excitement of the stormy sea, feeling the brave vessel fighting her way over and through the waves. She could do eleven knots and the Captain was making her work for a living. Tom stood, holding firmly onto the railings beside one of the crew's small lifeboats strapped down on the starboard deck. He allowed his body to rock with the ship and watched for the next streak of lightening to light up the crests of the waves and the spectacular cumulonimbus clouds on the horizon. In front of him the grey canvas over the lifeboat flapped with the wind.

It was when a flash of lightening coincided with the flapping of the canvas that Tom realised that he was not alone. He froze and waited, looking fixedly at the lifeboat in order to confirm his suspicions. The next explosion of lightning forked across the horizon and lingered. This time he saw it clearly. The face was pale and the eyes wide open. They were anxious and stared straight at him. If he was not mistaken he was in the company of a stowaway. Tom turned away to look across the sea. He needed time to think without alarming the frightened face under the canvas. He had a choice. He could either inform the Captain or ignore the situation and escape to his cabin.

Possibly against his principles, those of a law abiding and proud member of the small British community, Tom Reid did neither. Perhaps it was in memory of his own ancestor's beginnings in the Canary Islands when with a stroke of luck and great deal of risk they forged a life and fortune, that he chose a third option. He felt the need to know what had led the pale face in the lifeboat to be there before deciding what action to take.

In his mind, if no harm was being done in these circumstances, fair play and human need should override the written law. Times were not easy for local islanders. The economy was still struggling from the devastating effects of the Spanish Civil War and World War II. Many people were risking their lives by becoming illegal immigrants, some taking ships bound for North and South America. The Franco regime forbade it and anyone caught would be in serious trouble, mainly for political reasons.

Tom turned back to the lifeboat and when more lightening coincided with the flapping canvas he put a hand up as a sign of friendship. He held the rail with the other and eased slowly towards the frightened face. When he was close enough to touch the soaking canvas he smiled reassuringly. A finger was raised to the lips on the face as it pleaded to the interfering passenger not to give it away. Then both hands came up in a sign of prayer and dark eyes glinted half imploringly and half ashamed.

In reply Tom lifted the canvas very gently. He wanted to avoid any alarm but needed to see if there was more than one person in the lifeboat. Whatever he decided to do next the situation required mutual trust. The stowaway was alone. He was just a young lad. He could not have been more than sixteen. The boy was shivering with cold but managed to smile guiltily and shrugged his shoulders as if to say, "I've been found out!"

"Wait here!" Tom ordered quietly before putting a finger to his own lips as a sign of collusion and disappearing down a ladder and into the warmth inside. In the cabin there was a foul smell of recent vomit but his fellow passenger was snoring obliviously. Tom Reid smiled, grateful that the night's adventure was keeping him away from the stench. He put some biscuits and a flask in his raincoat pockets and stripped a blanket off the bunk before rocking, as clandestinely as he could, back to the lifeboat. He handed the blanket through the flapping canvas to eager hands and then took off his beloved London raincoat, doing likewise with it. Tom then casually wished the lad a Happy Christmas. The image of the boy's beaming face was to stay with him for the rest of his life. It was a picture of surprise and eternal gratitude. It was evidence of instant affection. There was no longer any need to know why the lad was there or if any member of the crew had participated in the plot.

"Eh, don Tomás!" shouted a voice from above. "Come up here *hombre* before you make me catch pneumonia thinking about you!" It was the Captain. He was in a good mood and ready to entertain his foolish English friend with a whisky and a warm bridge. It was time for Tom to bid the stowaway good luck.

The storm had moved on by the time Tom stepped off the La Palma onto the mole in Santa

Cruz. He had been permitted to spend the rest of the night in the crew's quarters and enjoyed a leisurely mid-morning breakfast with the Captain. Isidro, the chauffeur, was waiting for him beside the old black Humber. Just as the car turned away from the ship Tom saw a lanky figure waving at him from behind a lorry onto which wooden crates were being loaded. It was his friend, the stowaway. Tom told Isidro to stop. He got out of the car and stood on the cobblestones. The boy looked around briefly. He then came over to Tom Reid and began to take off the London raincoat.

"No, no. You keep it. It's yours now. Please, I insist!" That grateful smile again said all that was necessary.

"What is your name, *señor*? One day I will come and see you." Tom Reid offered his name in return for the boy's.

"I am called Alonso Valcárcel, *señor*. I am going to Venezuela". He had indeed been one of the thousands of Canary Islanders who found their way to Venezuela and to other South American countries in search of a better life and Tom Reid had simply offered a momentary helping hand.

In Alonso's case he had been smuggled aboard the La Palma by his cousin, a junior crew member. He had pretended to be a stevedore loading the ship with bananas and simply stayed aboard. In Tenerife he would either be found a job on a ship bound for the other side of the Atlantic or work in the port until he had saved enough money to pay for a berth on one of the many private vessels which were clandestinely ferrying islanders to South America in return for a considerable sum and in precarious conditions. As always, he made his own luck by using his charm and initiative to work his way across the Atlantic as a cabin boy on an old Italian liner called the Urania II.

Half a century later Alonso Valcárcel returned to the islands a very wealthy man. Sadly he was never able to see Tom Reid again, but he was determined to repay Tom's gesture on the mail boat in some way.

It took one or two brief enquiries and a visit to the British Games Club in Puerto de la Cruz for him to make contact with James and his own young family, and there was instant rapport between them.

"Here, I've something for you", smiled Alonso taking a parcel out of the boot of his car after lunch. "It belonged to a friend. Open it when you get home".

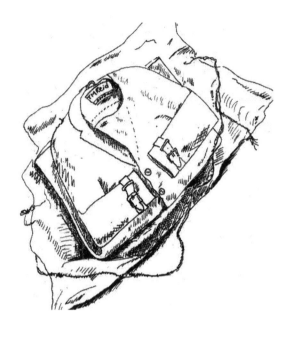

The brown paper parcel contained a very old and excellent quality London raincoat. The name T.M. Reid could be made out quite clearly on the lapel. In one pocket there was a pair of brown leather army gloves. In another there was an envelope with something I have promised never to disclose. All I can say is that it was Alonso's way of repaying the kindness he received all those years ago when he was a young and desperate lad, and for the foreigner's silence one cold and stormy night on the mail boat called La Palma.

THE PITANGA TREE

Alice was never permitted to set foot in the attic. It was the boys' room and her brothers defended it like possessive knights in a medieval castle.

The attic at Brambles, the family home in Surrey, was where they played with their trains and soldiers and, as they grew, where plots unfolded out of reach of little sister. It was also the natural store room for school trunks and forgotten things. To be fair, Alice never ever wanted to interfere with the boy's games. All she hoped for was a chance to peep inside one particular trunk, the one that never accompanied them to their boarding schools, the brown one in the corner. It had the initials A.J.C. on it which meant it must have belonged to her grandmother.

But in 1990 Alice got her way. Not only had she been given her grandmother's name. She also inherited Brambles, together with its attic and the brown trunk. Before her own boys took over the attic for themselves she got her husband to break open the padlock on the trunk. To begin with she was slightly disappointed. It was not filled with treasures or with the secrets that had so filled her daydreams as a girl. Inside she just found ordinary things like books, a bible, old photographs, a beautiful 1920s handbag, a lacrosse stick, a small African mahogany box and a bundle of diaries dating from 1930. Her grandmother, who died suddenly when Alice was too young to remember, must have been fifteen in 1930.

Alice left the trunk as it was but took possession of the beautiful handbag and put the mahogany box on her bedroom mantelpiece.

She wondered what might be inside it but found no trace of a key to fit and soon forgot all about it. But she decided to look at one of the diaries. It aroused her curiosity because it was the only one sealed with a red ribbon. It belonged to 1932.

One night after supper she carefully untied the ribbon and the diary opened itself on the 12th April, where it had been marked with a dried red rose and by a loose, folded piece of paper. It had an amateur water colouring on it depicting what looked like a tennis court and steps in the background leading up beside a stone wall. At the top of the steps her grandmother had painted what looked like a tree with a mass of small green leaves and dotted with bright red berries. Barely visible pencilled writing told her that it was actually a badminton court and an arrow pointed to a point under the tree. Next to the arrow her grandmother had written "My love waits patiently behind the black stone under the Pitangas. Here hides the heart I left behind on the Atlantic island."

The diary told Alice that in early 1932 her grandmother, who was seventeen at the time, had been sent to stay with her cousin in the Canary Islands to recover from pneumonia and that the air in Puerto de la Cruz had been miraculous. It also told her that her grandmother had been put on a ship home to England earlier than anticipated. The diary made no secret of the reasons. After heavy storms in February Mount Teide was sparkling with a white cloak of snow, warm easterlies had set in and an early spring invited the birds, plants and flowers in the garden at El Nido, her cousin's home on a hillside in the Orotava Valley, to blossom in an array of spectacular sound and colour. The island offered a natural promise of charms, feminine and sensual, and the young English lady had become attracted to a young islander called Imeldo.

It was under the pitanga tree that it all began. The young lady, a perfect example of English beauty, was floating through the gardens and strolled up the steps behind the badminton court, tempted by the tree with the bright red berries. At the top of the steps she discovered a field of onions. Water flowed into it from a narrow channel which ran along the foot of a black stone wall behind the tree. She also came face to face with the most handsome boy she had ever set eyes upon. She described a tall, olive skinned lad with jet black hair and brown eyes that at first inspected her arrogantly and then smiled a rich smile that pierced right through her, making her tingle all over. He was picking the red berries from the tree whilst watering the onion field. She was about to turn back to hurry down the steps when the boy reached a hand up into the tree, plucked one of the fruit and offered it to her, imploring her to try it.

"Pitangas. *Están sabrosas*, they're juicy!" he promised before putting another in his own mouth, rolling it about and then spitting an enormous pip at a lizard which was sunbathing on the stone wall. Her apparent surprise at the taste, the freedom of the encounter and their spontaneous laughter led to daily, furtive meetings under the pitanga tree. It was not long before the gentle climate, conversations in sign language and forbidden looks led to a point of no return with Imeldo. Warning signs invaded the household at El Nido. It was decided that a rapid recovery from her pneumonia had been achieved and that Alice's grandmother should depart before she caught another more complicated kind of illness.

The young English lady and the islander were permitted a brief farewell. They met under their tree at the top of the garden steps. It was not a sad goodbye. Instead it was almost as if a kind of logic had overcome their deepest thoughts. They both appeared to have accepted the ending as if it were as natural as the spring. Like their first encounter, Imeldo reached up into the pitanga tree and offered her a fruit with those smiling eyes of his. Then, from behind the tree he brought out a small, simple reed container and gave it to her. He had evidently made it himself and the reeds were still green. In return she put her hands behind her neck, undid her pearl necklace and gave it to Imeldo. A tear did appear on their cheeks, but it was one of hope, for both decided to put the necklace inside his container and to place it behind a stone. It was of a slightly darker shade of black to the rest, in the wall above the water channel. It was their simple way of telling each other that perhaps one day they would meet again under the tree.

Soon after reading the diary Alice persuaded her husband that they should take a holiday in Tenerife and in April 1991 they all arrived for the Easter Holidays at the Miramar, a delightful family run hotel in Puerto de la Cruz. Alice enquired at the desk about a house called El Nido. It was well known and just a fifteen minute walk up the hill. So, leaving her husband and the boys by the swimming pool, she set off with a map and her grandmother's water-coloured sketch.

El Nido was charming enough but it was very run down. The croquet lawn described by her grandmother no longer existed. A villa had taken its place. The new owner was kind enough to show her the remains of the badminton court which was now full of cracks and overgrown by weeds and wild creepers. The gardens were no longer an enchanting array of colour. The steps behind the court were still there but had been walled in at the top. There appeared to be another villa on the plot where the onions grew sixty years earlier. Things had changed a great deal. However, peeping from above the stone wall at the top of the steps was a very green tree with what appeared to be dozens of red berries. It was still there! Her grandmother's pitanga tree! It was now in the garden of a house belonging to a Mr. John Livings.

That evening at the Miramar Hotel the lady at the reception said she knew Mr. Livings well. His family had been merchants in Puerto since the middle of the 19th century and she offered to telephone to inform him that she had guests who would like to meet him. Consequently, without hesitation, Alice and her family were invited to tea the very next afternoon.

"I believe we must be distant cousins", Alice told their host. "My grandmother Alice Carter stayed at El Nido in 1932". A black and white photograph album was brought out during tea and they found a picture of Alice's grandmother sitting on a bench by the croquet lawn.

After a very short time Alice couldn't wait any longer. "Who was Imeldo?" she asked.

"Good Lord, he was the old gardener. I'm afraid he died last year. He'd been with the family all his life. Why?"

After explaining, not without certain emotion, about her grandmother's diary, Alice was invited to see the pitanga tree in a corner of the garden. John Livings explained that *pitanga* was the local name for the Surinam Cherry tree which had its origins in the subtropical jungles of South America, and that some people made jams from the fruit. The tree was full of fruit, orange, red and dark purple.

Nevertheless Alice simply longed to taste her grandmother's forbidden fruit. She also needed to know if the secret was still hidden in the stone wall. Sensing the urgency of the moment, John Livings picked a couple of the riper, dark red fruit and enjoyed watching his new cousins sample their bitter-sweet juice. Alice smiled and asked for another. Her husband refused. Then they searched behind the tree and above the now dry and disused water channel. When they removed a slightly darker shade of black stone from the wall they discovered the reed container. It crumbled under pressure in Alice's hand. But inside was the necklace of pearls, and attached to its timeworn string they found a small antique key. But for a slight covering of rust it and the pearls were in remarkably good condition.

"That must have been the key to your grandmother's young heart!" said Alice's husband, trying to break the ice after a long silence. His casual remark opened the floodgates to what was a very tense and sensitive moment. Alice could not hold back the tears. "No darling", she replied not knowing whether to laugh or cry, "this is the key to Granny's mahogany box".

TEA AT THE HOTEL

Old fashioned ways and manners, or quaint expressions of eccentricity, are often sneered at in this modern age of rush and first come first served. But sometimes they can add a refreshing touch of charm or even educate a young heart struggling to endure the onslaught of what some people call progress.

Nevertheless there is simply no reason why the progress lacking at one or two hotels in the Orotava Valley in the early 21st century should have represented such a decline in even the most basic of standards. Indeed I felt quite embarrassed at first and then touched with sheer delight when I heard about Mr. Alec Frith, a retired Englishman who decided to follow in his mother's footsteps and visit Puerto de la Cruz a year or two ago.

Alec Frith had lived with his mother in London, in a secluded mews house in Kensington. Being a relatively quiet and unadventurous sort he had been a librarian all his life, and never left the nest, so to speak. However, she left him a considerable fortune and a Victorian education not even the television could disintegrate. She had always spoken with great affection and longing about the charms of the Orotava Valley and the delightful port of Puerto de la Cruz. As a young lady in the 1950s she had spent five years as nanny to the children of a local aristocrat. She never returned and could not have known how much everything had changed.

The bus from Los Rodeos airport dropped Alec Frith and his suitcase on the road outside his hotel and he dragged himself and the case up the steps to the reception. There was no porter. The receptionist was staring blankly at a computer screen, which puzzled the newly arrived guest as the screen appeared to be blank as well. This was neither the Ritz nor a luxury monstrosity in the south of the island. In fact, it was just what he had asked for, a quiet hotel set in lush gardens away from the town centre din. There was such a silence that he picked up his suitcase and carried it to the lift. He didn't want to disturb anyone by wheeling it across the marble hall. Alec Frith was pleased with the view from the balcony, with the cleanliness of the simple room and with the adequate selection at the buffet dinner that evening. He had never travelled so knew no better. But he had expected a porter. To be fair the hotel was reasonably comfortable but a little worn and the next morning he rather enjoyed sitting under a small palm by the pool reading one of the books which had made his suitcase so heavy.

But his particular relationship with the hotel began on that first afternoon when he decided to take tea at the pool bar. An afternoon tea, as any Englishman will understand, is still terribly important. That, at least, is a tradition which progress has not managed to blemish.

"May I have a cup of tea please?" he enquired politely, removing his recently acquired straw panama hat.

"For wan or for tu?" replied the small, moustached man behind the bar.

"I beg your pardon?"

"You wan wan tea or pot o' tea?"

"Oh! A pot, please. Thank you very much", he replied, cursing his own stupidity.

Recovering quickly from the exchange Alec Frith sat down at a table under the shade of a leaning parasol. When the waiter brought the tray he poured himself what looked like very strong tea from a pewter-coloured pot into a plain white hotel cup. He then reached for the other pewter-coloured jug containing the milk before immediately wrenching his scalded hand back so fast that he very nearly sent everything flying onto the floor. He knocked the parasol's tube so hard with his elbow that it closed itself over his head, hiding the expression of pain on his face. He had never expected either the milk or the jug's handle to be scalding hot too. Being an educated fellow however he wasn't going to flick his fingers irritably at the waiter and went up to the bar. Nevertheless, his voice was more commanding and less grateful this time.

"The milk is hot, old boy!"

"Qué?" replied the man, much preferring to have even less to do that afternoon.

"The milk. It is hot. It should be cold."

185

After a shrug of the shoulders and an expression implying that here was another of those foreigners being a bloody nuisance, the waiter brought over a smaller container of cold milk and the Englishman duly completed the exact procedure of pouring himself a cup of tea. To cut a long story short, it was the most revolting cup of afternoon tea he had ever tasted and he only took one sip before putting on his panama hat and returning, rather irked by the experience, to his book under the palm. He didn't blame the waiter for his ignorance and assumed it must have been the kind of milk they used here which ruined his cup of tea.

The following morning Alec Frith found a grocery shop and bought himself biscuits, a carton of milk and a miniature bottle of Bell's whisky. He took these up to his room, went straight into the bathroom and emptied the whisky down the sink. He then thoroughly rinsed out the miniature whisky bottle and filled it with some of his newly purchased milk before putting it into the mini bar. That afternoon he took the miniature bottle of milk and a couple of biscuits down to the pool bar and ordered a pot of tea.

"Cold milk?" enquired the same waiter with a rather shrewd looking smile and with every intention of trying to please this time.

"No, thank you. No milk!"

The waiter lost his smile immediately and shrugged his shoulders. He then watched Alec Frith carefully pour the tea into the cup, take the miniature bottle out of a pocket and add a drop of milk, before placing two biscuits neatly on a paper serviette.

At first the waiter was fascinated by the expression of sheer pleasure on the Englishman's face. But then he almost took cover as if he were being shot at by marauding Berber tribesmen in Spain's North African colonies, where he had done his military service. Alec Frith nearly spat out the tea he had sipped and glared first at the tea cup and then at the waiter. When the Englishman opened the lid of the tea pot, spooned out the tea bag and began to read the label with an expression of disgust on his face the waiter rushed out to the poolside and pretended to empty ashtrays, mumbling *"Ay, Dios mío......ay mi madre!"*

The tea bag was of a kind of dark purple colour and had the words "best quality tea" across the bottom. It wasn't the milk. It was the tea!

At half past four the next afternoon Alec Frith strolled into the pool bar and looked at the waiter defiantly.

"Please listen very carefully", he said. "I want a pot of boiling water for two".

The man behind the bar pushed out his bottom lip and shrugged his shoulders as usual. The gesture not only implied that he would comply with the order but that he would not be held responsible for any further problems with the Englishman's afternoon tea. Then he watched with a remarkable expression on his face and presently nodded in a most understanding manner as Alec Frith took out two yellow Lipton's tea bags which he had bought at the same grocery store. He put them into the pot and waited for his tea to brew. Finally the waiter's face lit up with pleasure and he took full credit for the delight on the Englishman's face when the perfect cup of tea was sipped.

The same routine occurred on the following two afternoons and both the waiter, who kindly refused to charge the Englishman for his pots of water for two, and the guest seemed quite satisfied with the arrangement. They had solved their differences, both linguistic and cultural, and discovered they had something in common. They both had a murderous dislike of flies. The relationship became one of peaceful-coexistence and this led to a more concerted effort to be polite to foreigners in distress on one side and to be more understanding of pool bar attendants on the other.

However, a couple of days later Alec Frith was dozing under the palm half way through his holiday at the hotel when the kind waiter strode up very smartly indeed and informed him that his afternoon tea was ready to be served at his usual table. Rather taken aback and pleasantly surprised Frith followed the waiter to the pool bar, took off his hat and sat down expecting to be brought his pot of boiling hot water.

Instead, a tall, rather thin but elegant gentleman in his fifties appeared carrying a mahogany tray which he placed on the table in front of Alec Frith. The hotel guest was astonished to find not only a magnificent antique silver tea set but a bowl of sugar lumps, a selection of English biscuits and two china tea cups and saucers.

"May I join you, Mr. Frith?" asked a middle aged lady a moment later, before asking the tall gentleman to pour tea. "My family owns the hotel, and your dislike of our tea has been brought to my attention. I do hope you will accept my sincere apologies, but things are not as they once were."

The conversation was most agreeable and interesting. But something much more than a unique friendship developed the next afternoon. The Spanish señora had sent a note in the morning inviting Alec Frith home to have tea with her, and informing him that she would send Antonio, the same tall, thin, elegant gentleman who acted as chauffeur and butler, to collect him at four. After tea in a splendid drawing room, and a stroll through her extensive gardens, she took out an album of old, black and white family photographs. There was one in particular she was eager for the English librarian to see. It was of children and an attractive young lady sitting on a lawn.

"That's me when I was a little girl and those are my brothers. I'm afraid Alberto, the one on the right, died last year. The lady in the middle was Olivia, our English nanny. We were all so fond of her. She taught me how to pour a proper cup of tea and she made the most delicious scones. She wrote to my mother for many years after returning to England to be married," explained the Spanish lady with an expectant look in her eye.

"I know", replied Alec Frith. He then stood up and walked slowly over to the large bay window.

The lady of the house followed him and put a gentle hand on his shoulder, aware that her guest was evidently fighting back tears. After a considerable silence, he turned round, held both her hands and said, "This is quite a remarkable coincidence and one of the happiest moments of my life. Thank you so much. Olivia was my mother!"

THE PINK STRADIVARIUS

Penny Lattimer had just spent two long hours at the Herreros store in La Orotava looking for the last of the linen she required and buying new shoes for her two teenage boys, when the heavens opened and it began to pour with rain.

They attempted to run down the slippery cobbles in the direction of the car which Penny had parked by the square outside Anita's cake and tart shop, but the downpour and cascades from the rooftops turned the street into a torrent. Realising it would be futile to carry on without being drenched, and not having thought of bringing umbrellas, they stepped into the portico of an old town mansion.

It was early April 1966 and they had only recently arrived to live in Tenerife. Sam Lattimer had been posted to the island in order to set up what was to become a very successful distribution centre for a major Japanese vehicle manufacturer. Penny had been recommended the shop in La Orotava for the quality of its imported English goods. The two boys, Jamie and Peter were 17 and 15 respectively and would soon be returning to school in England for the summer term. New school shoes had been at the top of the shopping list ever since Easter term finished.

They peered through a wrought iron gate into a central patio. It was a beautiful entrance to what Penny realised was one of the town's many grand and sumptuous houses which she had been told about. It was lush with potted ferns and there was a delightful Roman fountain with water falling down into a stone pool. The rain ceased as suddenly as it had arrived but instead of stepping out into the street again Penny and her sons were captured, not by the hypnotising sound of water in the fountain, but by Beethoven. A piano was accompanying a cello from a room somewhere above.

After a few moments Penny, who had been a cellist at the Birmingham School of Music just after the war, exclaimed "Good God, I can't believe it. That's got to be a Stradivarius. Just listen to the vibration. Nothing sounds quite the same."

The sun began to shine through the gate and sent shivers through the boy's mother. She stood paralysed by the perfection of the music and her memories of days gone by. But her trance was quietly interrupted by a maidservant dressed in black and white uniform. She opened the gate and bade them enter.

"*Pasen por favor*. Please come in", she said leading them up a wide wooden staircase to the right and onto a gallery which overlooked the central Spanish patio. The music came from the other side of the house but the Lattimers were taken into a huge living room with exquisite French furniture and walls covered with glorious oils and delicate water colours. With the little Spanish they had learnt they understood from the girl that *la señora* would be with them in a moment.

"I am terribly sorry to have kept you waiting but I was still in my dressing gown when you took shelter in my porch. I am Antonia Montelugo. Would you join me for coffee?" As Penny Lattimer discovered in the following years, only someone educated by an English governess, as so many wealthy islanders were in the early to middle part of the 19th century, could speak such melodious and distinguished English.

The cello was being played by Emilia, her youngest daughter. She was just fourteen and practicing with her music teacher for a forthcoming concert.

"You must meet Emilia and I know she would just love to know you boys!" said Antonia with a wicked twinkle in her eye.

Of course that was the last thing Jamie and Peter wanted to hear. Trying to make polite conversation was not on their list of priorities after a morning shopping with their mother. But they were well brought up lads, smiled sweetly and followed the Spanish lady and their mother to the music room. They peered through the doorway until invited, reluctantly on their part, to interrupt the lesson.

It was another huge room but its ornate ceiling needed considerable restoration. There were no works of art hanging on these walls and the paint appeared to have been peeling off for years due to the damp. Two violins lay in their open cases on an old wooden table, another cello stood against the wall between the windows, and percussion instruments and an old guitar sat on very bohemian looking armchairs. The sunlight played with dust particles floating in the air to the melancholy sounds coming from the cello. An elderly lady at the piano concentrated on the music sheet in front of her.

Emilia continued to play, not once looking up, and a mass of chestnut hair fell gracefully over both shoulders and behind the cello which she balanced tenderly between her knees.

The sounds she produced by drawing the bow back and forth, and her smooth shifting technique on the strings would make even the toughest of men surrender. Then perhaps it was how she wore a loose man's jumper which came to just above her pale and rounded knees, or the sight of her bare feet on the wooden floorboards. But when the piece finally came to an end and Emilia looked up she left both boys knowing that there might one day be something much more interesting in Tenerife than the beaches. The girl they didn't feel like making polite conversation with was stunningly beautiful.

Penny, on the other hand, left Antonia Montelugo's house feeling slightly disappointed. It can't have been a Stradivarius after all, certainly not with all those pink engravings on the cello. The boys didn't see Emilia again during those Easter holidays and before they knew it they were on their way back to school on the British United Airways flight to Gatwick.

"I'm going to marry her!" Peter informed his older brother as the aeroplane descended over the Isle of Wight. Going back to school always made them look back at the holidays with a kind of empty stomach feeling. They were both wearing their new shoes bought in La Orotava and the conversation had taken them to the girl with the cello.

"I've got a much better idea" replied Jamie. "Perhaps Mummy was right and it is a Stradivarius. I'm going to pinch it and bring it to London. I could sell it. It might be worth a fortune!" Like any other brothers they were very different. Peter was always day dreaming and in love with somebody. Jamie wanted to be a millionaire and would stop at nothing, or so he liked to pretend. In fact he could never be a thief, but always took up a challenge and liked to shock his brother. Nevertheless he was going to be captain of cricket this term at Allhallows

School in Devon and thoughts of cellos soon drifted away. He would soon be far more interested in using his well known tactician's mind to defeat the best of England's public schools on the cricket field.

Funnily enough it was Jamie who eventually won the heart of Emilia the cellist when she was nineteen and he a graduate on holiday at his parents' home in Puerto de la Cruz. By that time the cello had gone. Emilia's father died leaving considerable debts for his family to deal with. As was the tradition, everything except the family home was sold. Young Peter Lattimer went to Sandhurst and became much more interested in war games. Jamie got a job with Lloyds and married Emilia. They went to London and lived in a small flat in Gloucester Road but hopped back and forth to Tenerife. After a number of years looking after many of Lloyds' Latin American clients as a result of the Spanish he had learnt in Tenerife, Jamie became an independent and very successful broker. He always knew he was going to make a fortune. They moved to a lovely house in the country and sent their children to boarding school, all three starting at a prep school called Cottesmore, which was conveniently placed very near to Gatwick airport in beautiful Sussex countryside.

In spite of Jamie's reputation for planning almost everything he did in life, his marriage to Emilia was a happy one, except for one year in the early 1990s. A stressed husband, children in their teens and the death of Antonia Montelugo got the better of Emilia. She moved back to the old family house in La Orotava to have what she referred to as a sabbatical. Jamie, who began to live more and more in their Gloucester road flat again, never failed to telephone her every evening. But he realised he would have to do something to stir his wife out of what was evidently the beginnings of a depression which she disguised extremely well. The most important business he would have to attend to from now on was ensuring his wife's happiness and his family's unity. That Christmas would have to be very special indeed. It was late October and he was gazing out at the autumn leaves in the park from his office when an idea caught his imagination.

Jamie telephoned an old school friend, Philip Schofield, who looked after the antique instruments department at Bonhams. Had he ever come across a pink Stradivarius cello? No, of course he hadn't. How ridiculous.

Nevertheless, the telephone rang two days later. It was the friend from Bonhams. It wasn't a Stradivarius but Philip had located a cello matching the description at McPharlin Guitar and Violin Company in a small town called Harmony in Pennsylvania. In fact it was described as a fine 1760s English cello by Joseph Hill. There were unusual engravings on the instrument's edges and scroll which had been tinted pink for some reason. That is why it was for sale for just under twelve thousand dollars.

Jamie booked five seats on the flight back to Tenerife for the family Christmas. Four were for his two sons, his daughter and himself. The other was for the pink Stradivarius. Today, people sheltering from the rain in the old portico in La Orotava still gaze placidly at the water falling from the Roman fountain in the central patio. Those lucky enough might also hear Beethoven coming from a room above, but only when Emilia is at home to play her cello. She is usually to be found wherever life takes her husband, Jamie Lattimer. As far as the pink tinted engravings were concerned, Emilia eventually owned up. When she had been an innocent twelve year old, unaware still of the value of certain things, she had used her first pink nail varnish to decorate the engravings on her beloved cello.

ABOUT THE AUTHOR

John Reid Young was born in London's Welbeck Street in 1957. Although he has spent most of his life in the Canary Islands, home to his paternal ancestors since the middle of the 19th century, he was educated at private schools in England and Scotland. Having first intended to go to Sandhurst he joined the Royal Navy for a brief period in 1976. He admits he entered the service as a rather immature schoolboy unready for hard work. Consequently it was a disaster. He always regrets not giving it another shot a couple of years later. After enjoying a few years working for a subsidiary of G.K.N. in Shropshire he was still determined to serve his country in some way. He tried on numerous occasions to join the British Diplomatic Service after going to university as a mature student and obtaining a Master's degree in Diplomatic Studies. He even got himself an interview with the SIS in 1988. A year later he returned to the Canary Islands. He is now a family man and enjoys nothing more than swimming in the Atlantic Ocean with his sons, playing tennis and gardening. He makes a living working for a small firm. He also gives private English lessons, translates documents for numerous clients including the regional parliament and contributes to local newspapers.

26890148R00119

Printed in Poland
by Amazon Fulfillment
Poland Sp. z o.o., Wrocław